Quotes from

Closure of the Helpdesk—A Geek Tragedy

"You want to know what happened to these Wall Street analysts? They've all become so obsessed with reading between the lines that they've stopped reading the lines."

"Come on, you want the big guys to approve this plan, not understand it!"

"That's exactly the problem with any 'simple truth'—in the end it always takes a gaggle of complete idiots or a team of all-knowing geniuses to miss it."

"Never lose time in sending the scapegoat to the slaughterhouse."

"Numbers don't lie. But people can lie about the numbers."

"In America, the glass is neither full nor empty. It is buy one, get one free."

CLOSURE OF THE HELPDESK

A GEEK TRAGEDY

Ali Sheikh

Anikini Inc.

Closure of the Helpdesk—A Geek Tragedy
Ali Sheikh

Printed in the United States of America.
Published by Anikini Inc.
www.anikini.com
For more information about this book, visit:
www.closureofthehelpdesk.com

Edition ISBNs
Trade Paperback 978-0-9885128-0-1
e-book 978-0-9885128-1-8

First Edition 2012

This edition was prepared for printing by The Editorial Department
7650 E. Broadway, #308, Tucson, Arizona 85710
www.editorialdepartment.com

Cover art by Carol Ruzicka
Book design by Christopher Fisher

In memory of my mother

Closure of the Helpdesk

A Geek Tragedy

Doughnuts Beat People

"The helpdesk is closed, Sam. You're on your own now."

"Stop kidding me, dude. I've got work to do." Sam moved closer to the phone and readjusted his headset. His long hair always got tangled in it, but that was the least of his problems on that day. He dialed #9 one more time in the hope of talking to someone—a real person—at the helpdesk.

"*You stop* hitting #9, dude," Vick said. "There's no one in there, I'm telling you. Not anymore."

Outside the drab offices of Bodega InfoTech on San Bernardino Avenue, it was a warm, sunny day. It was the kind of day when men across America would leave the office early to catch a ballgame. It was the kind of day when women would step out of the office around noon to meet girlfriends at a patio café for lunch. It was just the kind of day when pharmaceutical companies across America would routinely shoot and file away stock video footage of dreamy-eyed young people walking through picturesque meadows so they could continue selling their allergy medications to the unsuspecting public. But inside the drab offices of Bodega, Sam slouched in his chair angry and disheartened, as if his life had left him in a moment, with gloomy visions of going through the day without doing anything worthwhile.

"A lot of people are having network problems today," Vick said. "So you aren't alone."

"So the whole neighborhood is on fire, not just my house. Is that supposed to comfort me or what?"

"Relax, dude. Worse fates have fallen on us before."

Sam sighed. "I skipped breakfast so I could show up early and get some work done. Now I can't work. And I'm hungry. Sorry, man. I must've been taking it all out on you."

"I saw some doughnuts a while ago. In the pantry, I think," Vick said.

Sam got up from his chair. "The whole thing sucks," he said. "I wonder how many hours are being lost around here today just because no one is around to fix a little glitch in the network."

"Everyone is cutting costs these days, in case if you haven't noticed. They had to do *something*."

"Thanks for the news flash, dude. But what exactly were they trying to save anyway? Tech support isn't top dollar, right?"

"*That's* an interesting thought," Vick said. "So the next time Barbara or George come to *you* for advice, tell them just that."

Yeah right. It had been months since Barbara had approached Sam for his input on anything. The CEO still heard him out when *he* approached her, but that was about it. As for George, it was a whole different story—the CFO practically lived in a parallel universe.

"Oh well," Sam said, "looks like the day is ruined already. So much for showing up early to work."

"All isn't lost," Vick said. "You still got free doughnuts. Live for the little joys of life, my friend."

Sam's hunger pangs came back in an instant. He wandered away to the pantry looking for the much-needed doughnut. There weren't any in there, so he poured himself some coffee and continued the hunt. Sure enough, he found some near a meeting room. They were the usual assortment, all dunked in sugar or something equally sinful, neatly arranged on a small table at the entrance. There were two large flasks of coffee next to the doughnuts, along with Styrofoam cups and paper napkins. The room was vacant, with a large projector on the table and a laptop next to it.

Sam instantly deduced that an overpriced consultant was about to sell everyone at Bodega on an overrated idea. He visualized a three-hour-long meeting with a forty-slide presentation that said "NEW HORIZONS" on the first slide. In Arial 44 bold capitals, no less. And it probably had an italicized subtitle to boot, touting a shockingly new idea that would promise much only to fizzle out in six months or less: *e-vending—connecting vending machines to the Internet.* Or something like that. It didn't really matter what the rest of the slides said—you could fool all of the people all of the time, provided you brought doughnuts to the meeting.

He bit into his doughnut.

Krispy Kremes—the cornerstone of any nutritious breakfast! Sam played out a variation of *Pulp Fiction* in his mind. He further imagined finishing off the doughnut, washing it down with "hmm-that-hit-the-spot" office coffee and shooting at the managers. Reality soon caught up with him as he realized the managers weren't there yet. And the fact that he'd never owned a gun didn't seem to help much either. All he had was long hair à la Vincent Vega. He didn't quite fit in.

All the same, he was pleased with his reenactment of that hallowed scene from Hollywood, and with the fact that he could get something to eat. His hunger pangs started to subside, and the gradual realization that *he* wasn't among the hapless helpdesk guys who had just been laid off began to lift his spirits a bit. He wasn't a network maintenance guy but a senior architect, and a good one at that. Way more valuable and downright irreplaceable.

Sam went back to his desk, launched the control panel on his desktop and tried to repair his network connection. When that didn't work, he replaced the network cable, which didn't work either. He kept checking anything that came to mind, and within ten minutes he was out of things to check.

He looked around for Kris or Jennifer to see if they could help, but they weren't there.

"I don't know about Jen," Vick said. "Kris wanted to focus on bug fixes today. He's sitting upstairs so he can work undisturbed."

Sam wanted to go upstairs and talk to Barbara about the helpdesk, but he knew she was reachable only after lunch on Mondays. Nevertheless, he started playing out on what to say. *Barb, we really need the helpdesk.* No, that wasn't going to work in the middle of all the cost cutting that had been going on for months. *Remember, Barb, helpdesk was my idea and you were with me then.* No, that wasn't going to fly either—Barbara might think he was irrationally holding on to some pet idea from the past. *Barb, look at the productivity losses all around. The helpdesk actually saves money.* Yeah, that could work. But what if she wanted him to *quantify* things? Were there any metrics he could use?

Sam finished his doughnut, leaned back in his chair and did some mental math to see which cost his employer more, supplying free doughnuts or supporting the helpdesk.

"Doughnuts beat people," he blurted at Vick.

"Huh?"

Sam hastened to explain. "See, I've been running some numbers. Turns out that giving out free doughnuts costs us about the same as supporting the helpdesk. So, we could've kept the helpdesk, or we could have kept the free doughnuts. As it turned out, the doughnuts won."

"Um-hmm."

"Do you think we chose wisely, man? I mean, if a tech support guy showed up here and said, 'Please, please forgo the free doughnuts and in turn you get to keep me around,' wouldn't you choose him over the doughnuts?"

"No way. For starters, the tech support guys were never as sweet as doughnuts—"

"Now you're taking all this to a whole new level. In any case, can you imagine how it must feel to compete and lose out to a *doughnut?* That's what life has come to these days."

Vick nodded and turned back to his monitor. Sam decided to leave him alone.

Barb, the helpdesk costs the same as doughnuts. Can we bring it back? No, that wasn't going to work either. The CEO types needed a serious metric. A funny metric was by definition a useless one, even if it was accurate.

Relief came a little after 11, in the form of Jennifer. Though a hard-core programmer just like Sam and Vick, like always she knew better. After a few checks, trials, blind lanes and brainwaves, she spoke the magic words:

"Sam, did you change your log-on password at a time when you were *not* connected to the Bodega network?"

"It's now official," Sam told her with a bow, "you're a genius."

"Oh, that's been official for a long time," she said with mock haughtiness. "Well, now you know what to do. I've got to go."

It wasn't long before Sam regained his status as a living, kicking member of the connected world. He began passively reading though his e-mails and then browsed the net for a while. He needed four or five uninterrupted hours to work on his code, and it was already half past 11—much better to get the real work done right after lunch.

Seven hundred calories later, he came back happy and satisfied, with visions of making some solid progress through what was left of his day, only to discover that he was in receipt of an invite from Ted for a mandatory meeting that would take up most of the afternoon. Historically speaking, Sam had always reacted to meeting invites pretty much the same way the disaster management workers in the Deep South reacted to a rising Mississippi. And this one, like a Category 5 tornado, had come with no warning whatsoever.

"Imagine, an invite for a mandatory three-hour meeting with less than fifteen minutes' notice," Sam said. "A generation from now, Amnesty International will list this as a cruel and unusual punishment. The FBI will be forbidden from sending meeting invites to suspects during interrogation."

"Dude."

"Man, I don't know how you can take these things so calmly."

"Oh, I read math puzzles before I walk into a meeting," Vick said. "Then I sit there quietly and solve the puzzles in my mind. That's why I don't get worked up about these things."

"Okay, I get worked up easily—I give you that," Sam said. "But today, it isn't just this invite, man. It's the whole approach."

"Huh?"

"The whole approach to how they run this place. Look at what happened today. First, they ruin half my day by getting rid of the helpdesk. Then they ruin the other half by inviting me to yet another pointless meeting. Yeah, yet another useless meeting is just what we need… Frankly, I've had enough! I'll straighten all this out with Barb right now."

"And tell her what?"

Sam swallowed. *Deep down, I care about Bodega. I signed up because I believed our work had a purpose. I toiled here for two years because I thought we were changing the world, no less. But look around, Barb—all we do these days is run this company into the ground day after day, week after week, month after month.* Yeah, that's what he was going to tell her.

He went upstairs and started walking toward the CEO's office.

"Just the man I wanted to see," Barbara said as he walked in. "I've got only a minute, so I'll keep it brief. Did you get the meeting invite from Ted? I wanted to make sure you're attending."

"Barb—"

"Did you get the invite?"

"Yes."

"Good. Come talk to me after the meeting, around five o'clock. It's very important, okay?" She looked at her watch. "Now, if you'll excuse me, I have a meeting with George."

Sam returned to his cube shaking his head.

"What happened?" Vick asked. "Mission accomplished? Effective immediately, no more meetings at Bodega?"

"Dude."

"Okay, I'll shut up and let you vent. As long as you're the one buying beers this evening."

Sam told him what had happened. "You know what's odd? It's been months since she specifically asked me to attend a meeting. What do you make of that?"

"This could be important," Vick said. "Maybe our whole lives will revolve around it in the months and years to come."

"You're kidding, right?"

"Yes. And by the way, it started two minutes ago."

7

"Yikes! Let's go."

When Sam and Vick rushed into the conference room, everything was in place: Many of the technical architects and senior programmers were already there, the air conditioning was set high, and the lights were out save the cool beam of blue light from the projector. Ted was standing at the head of the conference table, chatting with Eric.

And there it was on the pull-down screen. In Arial 44 bold capitals, no less: "NEW HORIZONS." It even had an italicized subtitle to boot, touting a newfangled idea that positively shocked Sam on that day—he stood there in total silence for several seconds, reading the subtitle over and over.

"Are you all right?" Vick whispered to him.

"But," Sam said, his eyes fixated on the screen, "that's *my* idea."

MISSION CONTROL

GEORGE SAT IN HIS OFFICE behind closed doors studying the latest cash flow statement. He stared at the page for several seconds as if the numbers would change if he looked at them long enough. But there were no two ways of looking at those numbers: *situation not good.*

George didn't meet people unless he had to. Like they'd taught him in business school, operations guys were paid to holler, marketing guys were paid to talk and finance guys were paid to keep quiet. And the quieter he became, the faster he rose. He was made vice president of finance at Interstate Logistics by the age of 36. Then he was roped in by his long-term colleague and boss Barbara to be the CFO of Bodega after she'd quit Interstate to sign up as the CEO at Bodega.

In George's book, there was one more trait, apart from being quiet, that marked a good CFO: a singular focus on cash. All through his career, he worried—in good times and in bad times—about cash. More than profits. More than revenue. Even more than the stock price. A business could ride out an economic storm or two without much revenue or profits. But without cash in the bank? No chance in hell. Firms *always* went bankrupt when they ran out of cash.

And the situation wasn't looking good on the cash front.

The cell phone rang. The caller ID said it was Tom. George glanced at the door to make sure it was closed and picked up the phone.

"I told you not to call me at this time," George said.

"I'll keep it short, George. Is this a good time to short Bodega? Just say yes or no. We can catch up later."

"No."

"Thank you."

George lowered his voice—even quieter than his usual—and said, "Don't do anything now. Situation is a bit dynamic."

"Okay. I'll tell Clara."

"Be careful."

"I never screwed up anything," Tom said.

Yes, that's why you have this job. "Of course," George said. "But you can't be too careful."

"Talk to you later."

He opened his briefcase, took out his private notes and reviewed them. The notes reflected many future scenarios George had painted for Bodega, including some worst-case scenarios. And no, it wasn't time yet to short Bodega.

But it *was* time for him to tighten his grip over the firm like never before. With the dotcom bust barely six months old and the financial wounds still raw, he saw his opening.

He reviewed his notes one more time and headed to the CEO's office.

"Just look at all those happy people outside, George," Barbara said, looking at the expansive cube farm through the glass walls that covered much of her office. "Do they know or care what it's really like to run this place?"

George didn't reply.

"Gosh, I wish to heaven I was one of those carefree types," she said. "You know, show up at eight, leave around seven and have a good time in between."

George refrained from pointing out that she *had* been one of those carefree types just a few years back, before she started to aim high. In many ways she was still that carefree type. Which was why she always looked to him for managing the back office.

"So how many months do we have?" Barbara asked. "Did you say six months?"

"Eight, actually."

"How bad is it?"

"I'm talking about *bankruptcy* here, Barb. We're running out of cash."

"My God! We should've raised even more money last time around. But to be fair, who could've imagined that the whole dotcom thing would blow up like this?" She stopped pacing up and down and slumped into her chair. It was only a little after 1 p.m., but she looked tired and ready to go home. "What now, George? What's the way out?"

"It's back to basics, really. We aren't generating any money internally, and nobody will lend us money. So there's no choice but to raise fresh capital."

"What are our chances in this market?"

"You don't want to know."

"Jeez."

"The tide has turned," George said. "Till now it didn't matter that we never made a profit, but now it does. They all want to see something lean and focused and results-driven."

"We *are* lean," Barbara said. "We don't have any of that excess head count now, right? Where are we on that?"

"I just got rid of the last of the helpdesks. Their bloody contract finally expired and I refused to renew it. Yeah, they're all closed now."

"See? And we've gained focus. Look at New Horizons. We've got a game changer here, don't you think?"

"Everyone is saying that bit about focus and game changers, and in our case, that probably *is* true. But all that talk won't buy us much these days. They want to see some numbers—and those numbers had better be in black."

"Amazing how cynical they've all become in a year."

Cynical isn't the same as realistic, Barb. George sat in his chair waiting for her to resume. When she remained silent for twenty seconds for the first time during the meeting, he decided to play his card. "Here's what I think."

Barbara perked up.

"Remember Eureka?"

Barbara's face fell. She turned weary and scared in an instant, just as he had expected. "How can I forget? How can I *ever* forget something like that?"

"I know, I know. But in the end, we did okay," George said.

"More than okay, I think. But do you really want to do it all over again? Jeez."

"Not quite the same but something along those lines."

"George, do you really want to go to bed day after day scared to death about what could happen the next day?"

"No, I don't want to. But we *have* to. It's either that or bankruptcy unless *you* can work a miracle and raise some cash… This is your last chance to save Bodega. We have to do something. Doing nothing isn't an option."

"My God."

After a few seconds of silence George said, "I'll come back to you in a couple of weeks with more details."

"George?"

"Yes?"

"Anything I can do to help?"

Yes, Barb, for a change there is something you can do. "Yes. I want all our top talent to work on New Horizons. It could very well be a game changer, as you call it. At least the idea has some promise, and that isn't a bad start."

"That's easy," Barbara said. "A lot of our guys should be transitioning to New Horizons anyway. Oh, that reminds me—I wanted Sam to lead the development. I was planning on telling him this evening, after he gets to know the details from Ted and Eric."

"I see… Well, as long as things remain under control, that should be fine."

"You don't really like him, do you?"

"I'm not here to *like* someone," George said, "It's my job to look out for Bodega's finances, and that's what I'm going to do. Which brings me to my second point."

"Go on."

"Let me handle all the cash management. Any decision involving cash should now go through me."

"But George, many people around here think you have far too much power as it is. Now you want even more control. What do you expect me to say?"

"You know what's at stake. At a time like this, finance must assume more control. It's either that or—"

"I know." Barbara's face fell again. "But a few guys on the Management Committee aren't going to be happy about it. There will be a lot of turf issues. I need to speak with Steve as well…"

"Barb."

"Okay, George, leave it to me."

"Thank you." George got up and gathered his papers.

"George."

"Yes?"

"You saved us before, and I hope you'll save us again."

"Trust me."

George went back to his office, closed the door and reached for his private notebook.

George called Tom that night. "Listen, I don't want anyone to short Bodega. Scratch any and all plans you have."

"Wow, that's quite a change of stance."

"Like I said, the situation is a bit dynamic."

"I guess," Tom said. "So what's next?"

"The stock will stagnate for a while and then go up."

"Go *up?*"

"You bet," George said. "When the time comes, I'll tell you to move in."

"No offense, but what makes you so sure?"

"Because I'm in charge now. Which part of 'Things are a bit dynamic' don't you get?"

"Hey, I'm not complaining. You know I love it when a stock sings to our tune."

No, it will sing to my *tune.* "Glad to hear it."

GENIUS LOVES COMPANY

SHOULD I HAVE WORN A SUIT TODAY?

Sam kept fidgeting with his papers even though they were in perfect order and kept glancing at his resume even though he had memorized every word of it. He was waiting in a small meeting room, clad in his usual attire: dark trousers, a gray dress shirt and an expensive mechanical watch perhaps to compensate for his otherwise ordinary grooming and appearance. He had cleared the technical interview that morning and been asked to stay so Bodega's CEO could speak with him for a few minutes. Always a good sign—and it also meant, more likely than not, that it would all come down to the usual key question.

Sure enough, Barbara asked the question three minutes into the interview. "I see you're already employed in a similar position at LA Financial," she said. "So why do you want this job?"

To any other candidate, it might have been a routine question, but to Sam, someone had just asked his reason to exist. Silicon Valley had always been the epicenter of all things cool, but as the world counted down to a new millennium, it all soared to new heights. When talking about the new economy, all the metaphors in the world seemed meaningful; even the exaggerations came across as evenhanded. When it came to investor mania it was "the new tulips boom," when it came to job prospects it was "the new gold rush," and when it came to being a disruptive technology, the Internet was the pony express, the railroads and the telegraph all rolled into one. Sam just *had* to be there.

"To me," Sam said, "it's all about the nature of work. My LA job is all about changing the look and feel of a few web pages. Silicon Valley is all about changing… *the world.*"

"Changing the world, huh?" Barbara smiled. "I hear that a lot in the Valley these days. And you're right in a way—Bodega *is* all about changing the status quo."

Sam knew he had the job.

"By the way," Barbara said, "the way it works here, you get to build your own team and lead all the way. We want you to *deliver.* We don't want to hear any excuses. Any questions?"

"Where do I sign and when do I start?"

"Whoa, you *are* eager to change the world." She laughed. "I guess we'll have to put you on Pandora then."

Sam stared at his monitor for what seemed like an eternity but couldn't figure out why the bug fixes weren't working. No matter how many times he tried, the program remained uncooperative, unstable and stubborn—as if it were a real person with free will. But then, if the work were any easier, he wouldn't have moved to Silicon Valley, let alone joined Bodega.

The Internet was changing how the programmers viewed their work almost as much as the programmers were changing how people viewed the Internet. From the dawn of computing all the way to the late '90s, all the programs in the world had one purpose: to be run by a trained user during office hours on a given computer. But now it all had to run "seamlessly" even when complete strangers used unknown laptops in the middle of the night to access the most private of information stored on the remotest of machines. As always happens with any new-generation technology, one small mistake and it all came crumbling down.

As he grappled with the problem for hours, Sam began developing a love-hate relationship with it. As he had learned during his undergrad days, problems worthy of attack always proved their worth by fighting back. Sam hated the program when it fought back, but he loved it when it fought back in ways he hadn't expected it to fight back.

It was close to midnight and Sam was nowhere near to calling it a day. He hadn't eaten since lunch, and when he got to the point when he couldn't finish a thought without thinking of food, he headed for the pantry.

As he approached, a strong buttery aroma wafted out to meet him. When he walked in, a man who looked like any other geek at Bodega was microwaving popcorn. Unlike Sam, who was tall, athletic and well-groomed, he was a tad shorter and rather average-looking, with short hair and day-old stubble. He wore blue jeans and a white collarless T-shirt that read, "Got beer?"

"Hi," he said. "Want some popcorn?"

"Thanks." Sam took a handful and opened the refrigerator to look for a frozen dinner or a salad or even leftover pizza.

"There's nothing in there, I'm telling you. Popcorn is all we've got... Oh, by the way, I'm Vick."

Sam introduced himself, and the conversation soon drifted toward what was keeping them at work so late.

"The whole thing is so complicated," Sam said. "You touch one line of code and it all comes crashing down."

"Mind if I come over and take a look?"

"Are you sure? This is going to take a while."

"Why not? Worse fates have fallen on me before."

They went to Sam's desk, where they slaved for hours debugging the program. They cursed when new, unrelated problems revealed themselves, and they cursed even more as their hunger pangs grew with every passing hour. Finally, they figured out the root cause—a data type mismatch in a data transfer routine embedded deep in the bowels of an interface program—and fixed it once and for all.

Sam and Vick staggered out of the office a little after 4 a.m., tired, sleepy and happy.

"Why are we even leaving?" Sam said. "We need to be back at work soon."

"I don't know about you, but I'm hungry."

"I know a round-the-clock diner nearby," Sam said.

Between cheap bottled beers and even cheaper breakfast burritos, Sam filled Vick in on what Pandora was all about. Pandora was all about "middleware," the protocols, templates and programs for data transfers, system audits and error-handling mechanisms—the glue that held disparate computers together over vast distances. Middleware wasn't something an end user would ever see, but in a world where everything was being connected to everything else in new ways, nothing worked without middleware. As had been the case throughout the history of computing, the coolest lines of code were those that remained invisible to the user.

"Imagine," Sam said, "*for the first time in history*, all those super-secure corporate databases are going to be on talking terms with millions of customers across the world. What was unthinkable a year ago is now the *norm.*"

"That's an interesting project," Vick said. "Is there any chance I could—"

"Are you kidding? Of course you can be on Pandora."

"When can I start?"

"You started at midnight, didn't you?"

Everybody Loves A Good Problem

"Vick and I are already putting in 70-hour weeks," Sam said. "One more person on my team, that's all I ask."

"And so does every other team," Jane said. "You know what it's like to go on a hiring spree at a time when America has simply run out of smart people?"

"What?"

"Yeah, time was when I called the recruiters and said, 'We're hiring,' they were like, 'Thanks for calling us, Jane. We'll get back to you soon.' These days they're like. 'Okay, Jane, if that's your name, we'll see what we can do for you.' That's after I leave *four* voice mails. When I meet recruiters these days, *I'm* buying them lunch. What more can I say? On the top of it all, Steve doesn't want to hear any of this. He tells me I'm the head of HR, not him."

"Isn't he right, though?"

"That he's right doesn't help much. Oh, that reminds me— Steve is chairing a meeting tomorrow on this. Did you get the invite?"

Sam shook his head.

"Hmm… I really think he needs to hear from you," she said. "The way I see it, the problem is…"

"We've tried everything," Jane said. "Picnics in La Honda, day trips to Napa, harbor cruises in San Francisco. And we're still understaffed."

"I see," Steve said.

"The problem is we've been doing what everybody else is doing. I don't think that's the right approach. So let's do something original. Let's do what *really* makes our employees happy, not what we think makes them happy. Seriously, why are we taking everyone to Napa? Did our employees ask for it?"

"Oh, they don't like the free booze—is that what you're telling me?" Steve said. "That's the silliest thing I ever heard!"

"Actually, we don't," Sam said.

All heads turned toward Sam.

"You don't?" Steve asked.

Sam hesitated for a moment. He hadn't spoken in Steve's presence before. "We can buy the drinks ourselves right here instead of spending half a day on a bus ride into Napa."

"Go on."

"I think we should focus on what goes on *inside* the office, not outside."

"You have any ideas?"

"Here's a thought: You know how much time we all waste around here updating software, booking meeting rooms, hunting around for projectors and fixing laptops? My point is, these little things do get in the way of real work."

"So everyone should have a personal secretary? Is that what you're telling me?"

"No," Sam said. "We need, um, *helpdesks* so we all can focus on real work. When people are happy and productive, they stay on."

"Well, then, let's get started and see where it takes us. Ted, I want you to manage it. Ask John if you need any help."

"Sure," Ted said. "Let's have a meeting to discuss the specifics."

"What meeting and what specifics?" Steve said. "Whenever you're setting up a helpdesk, ask yourself a simple question: Does this make life a little easier for our employees? If the answer is yes, then go do it. I want to see *results,* not meetings, okay?"

"You got it."

"Sam, that's a good idea you brought up," Steve said. "But I want you to go back to your project and leave it all to Ted, all right?"

It all started with the two basic desks, the hardware desk and the software desk. Soon a support desk was added to deal with non-IT matters: telephones, headsets, projectors, facilities and the like. Then a mail desk was set up to take care of the two notable remnants of twentieth century workplace, documents and packages.

The game went up a few notches with the addition of the laundry desk, which made sense given that most dry cleaners closed by the time the average geek left for the day. Everyone liked it, though many made the expected off-color joke or two about doing one's dirty laundry in public.

Then a few middle managers—senior enough to have an office but not important enough to have a secretary—went up to Ted and made noises about how hard it was to make their own travel arrangements all the time, and in no time a travel desk was set up.

Having given the midlevel managers their midlevel perk, the top-level guys went in for a top-level perk: They started flying in chartered jets "to save time." Because booking a chartered jet was vastly different from booking cattle-class seats on a commercial flight, a new helpdesk was set up, which, being a paragon of efficiency, also handled the limo hires for the top guys. And because "chartered flights desk" sounded grandiose, they gave it a relatively egalitarian name: the limo desk.

Never a company to ignore its customers, Bodega also instituted a hospitality desk to whisk clients around when they visited, anything from the best shows in San Francisco to the obligatory limo ride to Napa and even an occasional round of golf at Pebble Beach. The employees were, of course, allowed to tag along for those "customer appreciation" events, which, of course, they did.

The desk that was most appreciated, from the top levels to the trenches, was the catering desk, a huge step up from the office cafeteria and the usual mass-produced monstrosities that passed for lunch. Employees simply stopped buying their meals—all they had to do was schedule a meeting around lunchtime and CC the catering desk on the meeting invite.

Sam sometimes got confused and called the support desk when he should have called the software desk. Senior employees almost always got the hospitality desk and the travel desk mixed up. Steve sometimes claimed there was a flowers desk when in reality it was the hospitality desk that was attending to his request.

Sam often joked that they needed a meta-helpdesk where people could go when they weren't sure where to go for help. And why not? "Help on help" wasn't an uncommon feature in the software world. He stopped joking about it when management actually sanctioned such a desk, the "common desk."

As the calls to the common desk poured in, they created a manager-level post for it, and gave it its own budget.

As the company added helpdesks, it also added talent and ended up with far more employees on its rolls than it had ever had. So Bodega expanded its home office on San Bernardino Avenue and went on a real estate binge, buying and leasing properties all over the town. As far as everyone was concerned, that was proof that the helpdesk idea had worked. Steve, Barbara and others would greet Sam jovially when they ran into him in the corridors; he was "that smart guy" who had come up with the idea.

"Sam," Barbara said one day, "just wanted to say I really appreciate you bringing in all these ideas. I don't know how far you got on 'changing the world,' but you've already brought in some positive change around here."

Sam blushed. "You're too kind."

"I mean it, Sam. Hey, whenever you need something—anything at all—come talk to me, okay?"

"Let's start with some good news," Jane opened the meeting. "The employee turnover has dropped for the first time ever. And I'm breathing a bit easy."

"Beautiful!" Steve said. "I *knew* helpdesk was a good idea the moment I heard it. Sometimes I get mixed up between limo desk and hospitality desk, but overall I'd say it was a good idea... So, Sam, did it work out all right for you guys?"

"Short of cleaning up in the morning, we don't have a thing to do," Sam said. "It's as if Bodega as a whole has become our helpdesk."

"That's nice to hear. Now if we could just find 300 more people, really smart people like you, I could start one more company just like this one." Steve began to complain, amid sympathetic oohs and sycophantic aahs all around, how in spite of everyone's best efforts, software talent was still hard to come by.

An hour after the meeting, Jane stopped by. "Sam, I'd like you to meet Jennifer."

Sam looked up. Standing next to Jane was a young woman. Probably, the finance department had hired her and she was being given a tour of all the other departments. She had the "finance" bearing for sure. She wore a business suit and stood tall and straight despite the heavy standard-issue Bodega laptop case she was carrying, reminding Sam of the women he had worked with at LA Financial.

"After all your help, I owe you one," Jane said. "And so here she is, your new team member."

"Team member?" Sam said. "No, it's more than that. She's the answer to my prayers!"

Jennifer stared at him.

"Uh, sorry," Sam added hastily. "My remark was purely work-related. I meant nothing beyond that."

"We aren't making a good start here, are we?" Jane said. "Just kidding. I know you two will get along just fine. See you later."

After Jane left, Sam showed Jennifer to an empty cube. "So, did they tell you that you'll hit the ground running?" he asked as she settled into a chair.

"That's the reason why I signed up. Where do we start?"

The (Java) Bean Counter

"Tell me again who approved all this," George said.

"Well, you know Ted approved it," Barbara said.

"What do you mean *Ted* approved it? Who allocates funds around here? Ted approves fifteen helpdesks on a whim and George is stuck paying the bills—is that our new financial policy?"

"George, George, it's not like Ted is overstepping your authority or anything. Steve told him to do it. I'll have a word with Ted to make sure he keeps you in the loop, okay?"

"It's not about being left out of the loop. It's about having a good handle on our finances."

"But…don't we have a good handle on finances? Don't we pay all our bills on time?"

Barb, it's positively moronic to spend money based on what you can pay now instead of what you actually make. But on the other hand, you aren't the only one in this country who does it all the time.

"George?"

"We pay on time, yes, but that doesn't mean much. It just means we've got truckloads of money to burn any way we please."

"I don't think we're burning money any way we please," Barbara said. "Don't get me wrong, I appreciate your input. But I don't think money is a problem."

"Let me ask you this," George said. "What happens when we use up all the cash? Have you thought of that?"

"That's where you come in. You keep track of the money, and if at any point it seems like we're going to need more capital, you come and tell me. I'll talk to Steve and get the money. He backs Bodega 100 percent."

Stopping by the ATM with Steve's debit card whenever you need money is no way to run a business, Barb. "It's good to know we have the backing," he said, "but that generally doesn't work in the long term. We need to *make* money."

"Don't get me wrong, I'm all for standing on our own feet and making money. But you have to spend money to make money. If we don't spend money, we can't retain our people. And if we can't retain our people, we have no product to sell. See?"

"So we open a helpdesk the moment a bunch of twenty-year-olds walk up to Ted and declare they're too busy 'changing the world' to do their freaking laundry? What's next, are we going to pre-chew their food for them?"

Barbara sighed. "They haven't asked for it, so I won't worry about it. Life is stressful enough as is. Look, Steve wants to retain top talent. End of the day, it's his money. Let's leave it there, okay?"

"Even if none of it is cost-effective?"

"And who's to say what's cost-effective? Just look around, George, and see what the other companies are doing. People are handing out the keys to a BMW on a soft loan. People are spending on junkets to Bali. *Bali, George!* Can you believe it? Lake Tahoe is so passé these days… Look, the whole Valley has gone so crazy that people are doing everything short of funding an all-geek cruise to the North Pole. Compared to that, a helpdesk here and a helpdesk there isn't going to hurt that much, is it?"

"So we aren't quite the fools because we're in the company of bigger fools? Barb, we really need to take this up with Steve."

"Steve isn't going to listen," Barbara said. "He wants operations guys to make decisions and deliver the results at any cost. Look, I shouldn't be telling you this, but he actually told me not to allow you to, um, interfere."

"Interfere?" George said. "*Interfere?* What did he really say—'Don't allow the bean counter to run the show'?"

"Steve values your expertise, George. He'd never talk about you that way."

"In the first place, I don't think that phrase is demeaning. No business can run without a bean counter. And in the second place, if it's the new economy or the digital economy or whatever the heck you want to call it, well then, I'm the *java bean* counter. I don't care if we're here to 'change the world'—a few basics never change."

"I told you where Steve is on this, George. What do you want me to do?"

For God's sake, stop doing everything Steve tells you to do and think on your own. "I'll think over what you said. And in the meantime, I'll continue to keep tabs on everything, and I'll come to you when I see something I don't like."

"Thank you, George," Barbara said. "Hope there are no hard feelings. Steve and I really like you."

"Glad to hear it."

IMMIGRANT EYE
FOR THE AMERICAN GUY

IT WAS A LITTLE AFTER 7. Sam and Vick were on their way out, absorbed in a discussion about how a seemingly irrelevant discovery today can make an amazing difference tomorrow.

"Take prime numbers," Vick was saying. "People who worked on prime numbers—Hardy, for example—conceded that their work had no real-world significance at all. Oh no, Hardy practically prided himself on that."

"Yeah, as if that was a virtue," Sam said.

"Anyway, the point is, we now use prime numbers for encryption. And I bet they didn't see it coming."

"Poor Hardy must be turning in his grave, cursing how useful all his work turned out to be."

"Ha-ha."

Through the corner of his eye, Sam saw Krishna, the new guy from India. From what he had gathered, Krishna had landed in America just a few weeks ago and worked with Team Icarus. Sam turned toward him. "Hey, Kris, you have the same prime numbers back in India?"

Even as he asked it, he regretted it. He'd wanted to be funny and friendly, but he was pretty sure his words had come out wrong. He was ready to apologize if Kris took offense, but it turned out he was taking it well.

He smiled. "Yes, we have the same prime numbers."

"Of course, of course," Sam said, trying to appear as friendly as he could. *I hope he doesn't think I'm some kind of jerk.*

"Actually," Kris said, "the prime numbers are the same no matter which country or planet or even galaxy and no matter which number system you use—decimal, hex, whatever."

"Dude," Vick asked, "are you saying any form of intelligent life, anywhere in the universe, any time, with any number system, will end up with the same prime numbers?"

"Absolutely. Take number 17 for example. Seventeen is a prime number not because we classify it as a prime but because it *is* a prime. That's why prime numbers constitute a surefire message. A message across time and space."

"A message?"

"Yes, a message," Kris went on, now visibly enthusiastic about this pet project he must have carried in his mind for some time. "Basically, you chisel the first hundred prime numbers into a granite stone and bury it deep. Take it to Nevada and bury it in your Yucca Mountain, for example. Ages later— I mean after the human civilization has all perished and aliens from outer space have inhabited the Earth—the new smart guys may one day go to the radioactive pile at Yucca Mountain in hazmat suits, and they may just dig up that stone and realize that once upon a time intelligent life existed on this planet."

"No kidding."

"You see, more than anything else we have ever made, more than those Pyramids in Egypt, more than all the nuclear waste in Yucca Mountain, that granite stone with prime numbers is the surefire hieroglyphic thing we could leave behind as a souvenir to the future inhabitants of this planet."

"Cool," Sam said. "Where did you read all this about Yucca Mountain?"

"*National Geographic.* It has quite a following among Indians. I once read an essay about how they measure water seepage through Yucca Mountain."

"What?"

"Yes—they need to measure how slowly the water seeps through the mountain. That's how they determine if all that nuclear waste can be stored there without damaging the environment."

Sam stood silent as his mind's eye played a few short futuristic video clips of water seepage in Yucca Mountain, prime numbers chiseled in granite and aliens wearing hazmat suits. That was one deadly combination of disparate things that hadn't dawned on him before.

Sam looked at Kris. All he saw was a friendly, eager-to-please face, with no trace of pretension or arrogance or even one-upmanship despite the winning discourse he had just delivered.

I've got to get this guy on my team. He asked Kris the all-important question: "There's a happy hour at Duncan's—want to go with us?"

"Evan did all the groundwork," Barbara said. "He found and interviewed Kris, he worked with the immigration lawyer and he got the visa done. Now you want him on *your* team? Tell me why. Does Kris bring any skills that are critical to Pandora?"

He wrote control software for turbines. No, that wasn't going to work. *Kris is a smart guy and I want him on my team.* No, that wasn't going to work either.

31

"What am I going to tell Evan?" Barbara asked.

Remember, Barb, you said I could come to you when I needed anything. No, he wasn't going to say that either. Sam hated putting people on the spot. That Barbara was the CEO was beside the point. "I can't tell you what to tell Evan," he finally said. "But I can tell you this: You put Kris on my team, I will deliver Pandora on time, no matter what."

Barbara looked up. "That's good. I think we can work with it."

"Thank you."

"Thank *you*. You may not always realize it, Sam, but I have a long list of problems. Good to know Pandora won't ever be on that list."

It's Called PANDORA
for a Reason

"Tell me," Vick said, "why do we call this Pandora when *we are giving it* everything we've got?"

"*Slacker*," Sam said. "You're supposed to give it everything you've got and then some. Next item on the agenda…"

They were at the team meeting that Sam chaired every Monday at 7 p.m. Like always, they had been working for twelve straight hours or more, and like always they sat at the meeting with the energy and attitude of people who had just shown up to work. But at least there was something to show—literally—for all that work.

They had presented a system demo to Barbara, Ted and John that morning. While everyone watched, Kris entered the data—a mocked-up customer purchase order—on a PC at the "buyer's end." Moments later, that order could be seen updating the orders and inventory data at the "seller's end." Sam did most of the talking, filling them in on what they were doing in terms of cross-platform integration, data security and performance tuning. Barbara talked at length about how pleased she was, peppering her conversation with *strategic* and *seamless*. John had only a couple of quick questions, and like always, Ted confined himself to nodding sagely whenever Barbara spoke. Not a bad meeting in all.

"Dude, are we done here?" Vick asked.

Sam shifted his attention back to the meeting. "Sorry," he said, "next item on the agenda: Does anyone need anything?"

"I need a new computer," Jennifer said. "Mine isn't fast enough."

"Come on," Vick said, "it isn't cool enough. Isn't that the real reason?"

"Either way, we'll get you a new one," Sam said. "Anything else? I mean, we barely made a dent in our 'goodies budget' this quarter."

"All right," Vick said, "it's time for extreme makeover, Silicon Valley version. A projector for our team, new chairs for everyone, twenty-inch monitors—come on, people, we're on *Pandora,* for God's sake."

"Espresso machine," Kris said. "Our own espresso machine."

"Whoa," Vick said, "I like the way you think."

"I was joking."

"Oh that's nothing," Sam said. "You guys know what *Ted* has in his office now?"

"A box of Legos?" Vick said. "I bet he's building a train station as we speak."

"Well, he got an aquarium, but I see your point."

"Ooh, an aquarium," Vick said. "My bad. Playing with Legos is hard work. Much easier to sit back and watch the fish."

"Anyway," Sam said, "what else?"

"A date," Vick said. "I'm far too busy to find a date all by myself." He laughed before Sam could respond. "Just kidding, relax."

"At least Kris won't have to worry about it," Jennifer said.

"So, have your parents found you a cute girl yet?"

Kris laughed. "No, it isn't always like that."

Vick turned toward Kris. "If what Jen says is true, that's one amazing helpdesk you got there. Can I call your mother? Maybe she'll set up me, too."

"Hey, you guys, leave him alone, all right?" Sam said.

"Oh, you want us to help *you* instead?" Jennifer asked.

"Oh, no, not at all." Sam blushed. "Let's get back to work, okay?"

The world was changing fast—arguably faster than at any other time in history when people said the world was changing fast. Day after day, the new economy supplemented more and more commonplace verbs with the all-magical prefix *e*. Week after week, the business press recycled the same "big picture" story, but always with a new sidebar on how yet another facet of life—anything from the most mundane of tasks to the most intimate of relationships—was being transformed like never before.

But on the other hand, the reality of working in the Valley didn't fall far short of the hype. And in the living-large department, it even measured up to the hype. If two people met in Lake Tahoe and exchanged business cards, the whole getaway was by definition a business expense. No meeting with a client was ever complete without a fancy meal on the company dime, and no all-day workshop was complete without wine tasting in the evening or a harbor cruise or, better still, wine tasting on a harbor cruise. All around the Valley, vitamin M could be mixed with anything, and like anywhere else, it dissolved quickly without leaving a trace.

While the perks were nice and the press coverage was nicer, for Sam the real happiness often lay in seeing how the project deliverables were shaping up. Barbara was happy with his system demos and the other deliverables in the pipeline—the performance benchmarks, guidelines for error handling and the administrator guides—were more or less on schedule.

Barbara often called Pandora Bodega's "most promising project" at the monthly review meetings, and Sam knew that a few potential clients were talking to Bodega about deploying Pandora on a pilot basis. Even Steve stopped and said hello when he ran into Sam in the office lobby.

Sam couldn't have asked for anything more—not even of Pandora.

What do you Mean "Money Apart"?

George read the report over and over. On the surface, it was the usual monthly report showing the amounts of money budgeted for projects and the amounts actually spent. Bodega's top brass had reviewed those numbers as agenda item 8 earlier that morning. No one spoke a word at the meeting, presumably because no one cared for the numbers or even understood the numbers. George, on the other hand, cared for the numbers and understood the numbers, which was *his* reason for not speaking up. Anything of significance was always done behind closed doors, with two or at most three people. Larger meetings existed only to share the decisions after they'd been made, if they were to be shared at all.

George looked at his watch. Time to meet Barbara, in every sense of the word.

"We need to talk," George said.

"Uh-oh, not a good sign." Barbara smiled. "Just kidding. Remember, that's what you used to say when things were about to go bad at Interstate. On second thought, scratch that. I don't want to talk about Interstate again. So what's up?"

"We *are* in bad shape, Barb."

"Oh, come on now. You were at the morning meeting yourself, and you know everyone is happy with how things are shaping up."

"Barb, we aren't making money. The rest doesn't matter one bit."

"Oh, not *that* again," Barbara said, shaking her head. "Come on, George, haven't we been through this before? God, you scared me there for a minute. Don't worry, I'll go talk to Steve."

"And ask him for what, a hundred million dollars?"

Barbara kept staring at him, blanched and speechless. George remained silent, waiting for her to absorb what she had just heard. For the first time since joining Bodega, he could hear the muted hum of the laser printer down the corridor.

"A hundred million?" Barbara finally asked.

George didn't reply. He sat across from her calm and collected, with his hand resting on his yellow notepad.

"How am I going to ask for that kind of money?" she said. "This is shocking, George. I didn't expect to hear this from you."

"Excuse me, but haven't we been through this before? 'Let the operations guys make the decisions, George. You just keep tabs on money.' That's what you always said. Well, all those operations guys and their big boy Ted have been partying like there's no tomorrow, and guess what—we need a hundred million to keep this party going."

Barbara remained silent, shaking her head as she looked down at her desk. "I don't know what to say," she finally said, her voice weak. "What the hell is going on, George? What am I going to tell Steve? He'll throw a fit when he hears it."

"If he hears it."

"What?" Barbara said, looking more confused than ever. "What…what are you saying, George?"

George sat quietly, with look of polite inquiry about him, as if to say, "Your move, Barb."

Barbara looked him in the eye. "George, I'm not going to ask Steve for a hundred million dollars. I need your help. And you know we're in this together."

"Barb, I really need to know where you stand. Frankly, I've been getting some mixed messages from you for a very long time."

"What do you mean?"

"*You know* what I mean."

Barbara sighed. "What do you want me to say, George?"

"Well, please collect your thoughts and identify the *root cause* of what brought Bodega to this. Once you've identified the problem and you're ready to act, we can talk."

"I still can't believe it," Barbara said. "I gave *Ted* full operational control—in good faith—so I could focus at the strategic level. Who could've imagined it would one day come to this?"

"*I know*," George said.

"I can't believe it… What took you so long to tell me all this?"

"Because I wanted to wait till I had some hard numbers to show. Now that I have the numbers, I'm sharing with you, even if they're troubling to know. Nothing personal. I mean, I trusted Ted like anyone else in this company."

Barbara shook her head. "Trusted Ted… I should've known better than to trust these empty suits… God, Steve is going to chew me out over this… George, you have a plan yet?"

"Three things. Are you ready?"

"I can't wait."

"First, ask Steve for *ten* million dollars. While you're at it, don't keep him in the dark; tell him how things have been going. When there's bad news, you should be the first to tell him. Second, tell him we should raise additional capital 'just in case,' to the tune of twenty million, or even thirty if we can wing it."

"I'll do that," Barbara said. "And what about Ted—should we let him go? Seriously, George, I can't get over how clueless he's been on all this."

Never lose time in sending the scapegoat to the slaughterhouse, I know. But on the other hand, Ted has his uses. "Well, you're about to raise thirty million. Firing your right-hand man at a time like this won't look good on you. So, you tell Steve you're going to assume more control, perhaps shift some responsibilities to me. Controlling the spending, reining in the overzealous executives, that sort of thing."

"I can do that," she said. "Anything else?"

"Yes, that brings me to my last point," George said. "Put a freeze on hiring. If anyone questions it, tell them we need to stabilize our operations before we hire again. Between you and me, we'll have to let go of a few people."

"But, George, I really don't want to upset the apple cart. We have so many smart people working on all these ideas. I mean, money apart, things have been running pretty smooth."

"What do you mean 'money apart'? When you're running a business, money isn't an afterthought. And by the way, you can't throw out the bad apples without upsetting the apple cart."

Barbara remained silent for several seconds. Then she looked up. "George, I want you to know you have my full support. Please tell me you'll see this through."

"Trust me."

"Good. I'll go talk to Steve. And I'll make sure Ted is under control."

George got up from his chair.

"Is there anything you want me to send out to the whole team?" Barbara asked. "At a time like this, we need to set the right priorities and communicate clearly."

"Don't send anything out. Let them keep having their fun."

"Really?"

"Yes. Our job is easier that way."

I IM, Therefore I am

"I've been thinking," Sam said.

Vick looked up from his lunch. "Ah, it's PWD time again?" With at least half a dozen other projects at Bodega that were supposedly changing the world, anyone wanting to establish some street cred had to have a whole portfolio of ideas that would change the world—a PWD, or program for world domination, as they called it only half in jest. The further the idea was from the "official" work, the cooler it was to brag about over lunch. It also helped that Bodega encouraged it—in fact the projects Icarus and Prometheus were practically drawn up at the cafeteria.

"No, it isn't just talk," Sam said. "I've been working on this. First, here's the big picture—"

"Oh, never mind the 'big picture,'" Vick said. "That's what *Ted* is paid to talk about. Dive right in, dude. What's the idea?"

"Mobile commerce. As in buying things from a cell phone. Look, why can't we buy movie tickets from a phone? Or do our groceries?"

"I can do that right now. All I've got to do is call someone and ask him to get the groceries or the movie tickets or whatever."

"Come on, you know what I mean. You should be able to do things just by pressing a few buttons on the phone. Imagine doing all our shopping on the phone while waiting in line at a coffee shop!"

"But why do you have to wait in line in the first place? Can't you order the coffee from the phone and walk up to the coffee shop just to pick it up?"

"Now *that's* an idea," Sam said.

"I was just joking," Vick said.

"I wasn't."

"Seriously. Isn't Pandora enough? You want to change the world all over again? In your spare time?"

Sam smiled. "That's the plan."

Sam sat in bed with his laptop on a breakfast tray and started debugging the code for the seventh time that day. Thanks to the wonders of technology, he didn't even need a cell phone in order to develop or test the program, much less a mobile phone network. Cell phone simulators were available, by way of free downloads, for any interested and capable developer.

Sam installed the simulators for a few phones from Nokia and Ericsson and started playing with WAP technology. The wireless application protocol was still nascent, but it enabled the basics such as navigating between screens and selecting menu options. For a few hours, he tried to simulate the buying experience on the tiny simulated screen on his laptop. He eventually completed a no-frills interface, starting with a "main menu" listing produce, beverages, condiments, medicines and other categories. The user could navigate into the beverages section, for example, select "sodas" and choose or drop an item by clicking the "yes" or "no" buttons on the cell phone.

Though happy with the progress, Sam knew there was much more to it. The cell phone company had to be somehow connected to the grocery store. And to the credit card company for payment. In the end, many disparate systems and technologies had to be brought together to make the whole thing work.

Disparate systems had to be brought together? Sam sat up in his bed as light bulbs went off all over. Why, the whole idea was nothing but Pandora in action. In hindsight, it was obvious why the idea had come to *him*. Yes, if there was one person at Bodega who could see it through, it was him. He could put in some more time, complete the design and take it to Barbara.

But on the other hand, Bodega was a *technology* company, not a consumer services company. In all likelihood, Barbara would tell him to focus on Pandora first. But on the other hand, if he waited till Pandora was wrapped up and then went to Barbara to show how Pandora could be developed further...

Yeah, that could work. He could take it to Barbara in a few months, and in the meantime he could work on it in his spare time.

But *time* was exactly the problem. He was already working fifteen hours a day, the code freeze on Pandora was barely four weeks away and last but not the least, the project audit was looming. Sam knew that audit was important—it would provide the much-needed validation for all the good work he and his team had been putting in.

***

44

"Don't you think I have a point?" Sam asked. "People *are* open to using their cell phones in new ways. Look how texting is catching on—I won't be surprised if people stopped talking altogether before long."

"Oh no," Vick said. "I for one like to *talk* to people, not IM them."

"What's the big deal?"

"Have you considered its impact on…the English language?"

"You lost me," Sam said. "What's your point?"

"Think about it. There was a time when English was all *bookish*. Then TV was invented and people started watching it all day, and then the era of television English was upon us, with tons and tons of dialogue. Any book published these days has tons of dialogue—did you ever notice that?"

"Ah, so you fear the era of IM English will soon be upon us?"

"Or it could even turn into a whole new language," Vick said. "*IMglish*, Sam! Imagine, whole books written in IMglish!"

Sam laughed. "OMG!"

"Hmm, 'OMG.' An ominous, attention-grabbing line that's full of promise and warns of imminent danger. It could serve as the opening line for a riveting page-turner, don't you think? As in 'OMG, my bff IMed.'"

"Stop it or I'll finish your beer."

"Point noted," Vick said, clutching his beer. "But when the angry masses revolt in defense of the English language and cell phones go all retro, out goes texting. And out goes your business model, too. See?"

"Oh well," Sam said. "I was really hoping to talk you into working with me. I guess that's not happening."

"But on the other hand, see those hot chicks over there? If our phones could figure out their numbers and auto-text them asking for a date, now *that* would be cool."

"That's one more thing we need to work on... I mean the chicks, not the phone."

"Thank God."

TRUE LOVE

"I DON'T THINK I'VE EVER GONE OUT with a geek before," Kelly said.

Sam smiled. Changing the world was the easy part. When it came to scoring a date, everything was working against him. The Valley had the highest proportion of single men to women in all of America, and working on Pandora—or anything else in the Valley—meant no time for a personal life. There was a self-imposed obstacle as well: Sam wanted to maintain a professional demeanor at work at all times. That ruled out asking out anyone at Bodega, even when the company policy said nothing, not even informally, about dating a coworker. But there he was, finally out on a date with the girl he had been chatting up online sporadically for three weeks.

"Dating a geek has its advantages," Sam said.

"Enlighten me," Kelly said. "You've been very quiet. If your plan was to come across as the strong, silent type, you're already halfway there."

"Well, we geeks are really simple people. When we don't know something, we openly admit it, and when we know, we tell it like it is."

"So you aren't a liar. Not a bad start, if you ask me. Is that what you wanted to tell me on our first date?"

"There's more. I looked up on what to say on the first date. Turns out you tell a pretty girl that she's smart and a smart girl that she's pretty. So I was planning to say you're the smartest girl I've ever met."

"Obviously, you're saying I'm pretty. Oh wait—if that's what you're *obviously* saying, you meant to say I'm smart... But wait—we've established that you aren't a liar, so I have to back up a bit and work that in... So you're saying, in effect..." She raised her glass. "You know, that's the most convoluted compliment I ever got."

"Well, I worked on it for a while, with a flowchart and a start condition."

After her second drink, Kelly asked, "Hey, you want to check out the new tapas place on Mimosa Avenue? It's nine o'clock now—there can't be too much of a wait."

Sam's face fell. He had slept for a total of nine hours in three days. He had downed a double espresso right before the date just so he could keep his eyes open. He wanted to go home and crash for an hour and then resume working on the code.

"Pity," Kelly said, "I guess you're tired or something."

"Sorry, but I have to work," he said. "I'll make it up to you next time, I promise. Drinks, dinner and movie, all on me."

"You're going to work *now?* Funny, I never thought you guys had anything like a graveyard shift."

"We don't. We just call it the workday."

Just when Sam had finally figured out how to manage the workload, out of nowhere the auditors from Sedona Consulting were brought in to "monitor project progress and ensure consistent development standards."

Sedona's fame preceded its engagement with Bodega. For starters, it had a brochure that liberally quoted Sun Tzu. It even ran a popular TV spot that opened with multiracial children playing at a preschool and ended with a breathtaking sunset in the great outdoors of Sedona. The tag line was a bit cheesy but nevertheless quite a hit among the geeks: "Sedona Consulting: We cast long shadows over the system landscape."

"Just great," Vick said when Sam told him of the upcoming audits. "We never had the time to finish the real work, and now we have to complete a truckload of documentation for everything we ever did, assuming we can remember what we did in the first place."

"That's the whole point," Sam said. "I'm all for it. It's a good thing, speaking from a quality perspective."

"What about the let's-get-a-life perspective? Overwork is nothing new around here, but really, Sam? On the top of changing the world, we're supposed to document *how* we're changing the world?"

"Look, I went up and asked the same question. There's a freeze on hiring."

"Ah, so the big guys want to keep their bonuses and therefore we have to work ourselves to death? When is this going to end? Oh, I know—it'll stop only when a nosy journalist visits our office and mistakes us for undernourished aliens locked up in a secret CIA facility, with Bodega serving as a front, and makes it a front-page story. Yeah, that's when. Wait—now that I say it, I'm not sure it'll happen even then."

"In the first place," Sam said, "you could say that about any company around here. Surely you don't think the whole Silicon Valley is just a front for the CIA. And in the second place, I'm going to share the workload, so it's not like I'm dumping all this on you."

"Dude, that's not what I meant."

"I know, let's put everything else on the backburner for a week and go through this, all right?"

It was 9:30 p.m. Sam sat in his bed, with his laptop on the breakfast tray and an untouched pizza on the nightstand, collecting his thoughts on his mobile commerce idea. He wanted to work on it for a while, but a quick look at his "to-do" list reminded him that he had less than ten hours to review a mountain of Pandora flowcharts and endless pages of test results. He wasn't sure how much sleep he could fit in, if any. But on the other hand, the project audit on Pandora was going well. He could tell that the Sedona guys were impressed with everything they had seen.

Stop fooling around with cell phones and groceries and WAP—Pandora is the true love here. Sam closed his files on the grocery shop simulator and started reviewing the Pandora charts.

He'd gotten through twenty pages when the phone rang. It was Kelly.

"Hey it's me," she said. "Where *are* you?"

My God—I totally forgot. "I'm so sorry," he said. "I've been working all day and totally forgot the date."

"I thought you made a promise."

"Kelly, believe me, it's an honest mistake."

"That's your third 'honest mistake.' Sounds like someone has his priorities right."

"Look, Kelly, I screwed up, okay? I'm so sorry."

"Okay, I'm buying the tickets now. You'd better make it here in twenty minutes."

"Look, I've got to work," he said.

"What?"

"Kelly—"

"Why did you even pick up the phone? Can't you just ignore my calls so I get the message?"

"Kelly, I'm not trying to avoid you!"

"Funny, I thought you weren't a liar."

"Wait, Kelly—"

She hung up.

Sam called her back immediately, his mind racing over what to say. It went to her voice mail. Sam hung up. *She's too upset, and I have no clue what to say...*

He sat up in his bed staring at the wall, wondering what was next. The silence was broken only by a ping on his laptop announcing the arrival of an e-mail. It was from Vick:

> Sam, could you review the enclosed spec and fill out the sections on performance considerations? I know you're super busy, but I have a feeling you'll make time. Admit it, dude, performance tuning on large-scale data migrations has always been your true love...

Sam looked at the clock. It was 10:30 p.m.

"I suppose I can do it," he wrote back. "I'm not going to get any sleep tonight anyway."

CHINKS IN THE ARMOR

GEORGE REMAINED DEEP in thought long after the Sedona guys had left his office. Just as he had asked, they had audited all of the fourteen projects at Bodega and filed their report. In many parts, its forty pages confirmed what George had always suspected, and in some parts it added the detail to what he had always feared. In the end, the report said, the majority of the projects at Bodega were not getting anywhere. Only three projects—Icarus, Hercules and Pandora—had good leadership, decent quality control and, most important, the promise of any future revenues.

Good starting point. Keep those three and kill everything else.

Like a military dictator who suspends the constitutional bodies right after assuming control, George first did away with the management oversight committees, the corporate coordination teams, the strategic initiative groups and anything else that resembled a governing body. Also thrown out the window were the vision, the mission, the values and all the related verbiage.

Then he turned his attention to the helpdesks. On day one, he got rid of half the helpdesks in one fell swoop. He continued till he was left with just one desk: the tech support desk, often called *the* helpdesk because of the high number of calls it answered on any given day.

"You can't fire them," Ted said. "First of all, they aren't our employees. Second, they're here on a long-term contract from Sequoia Support and we can't terminate at such short notice without paying huge termination fees."

"Okay then," George said, "keep them, but only till their contract expires. And fire the idiot who signed that Sequoia contract."

As he continued to cut costs, many of the middle managers fought back, just as he had expected. As George knew only too well, when you took away a man's budget, you took away his power. Even his dignity.

Particularly John's, as it turned out. Apparently, he was the hardest to crack. Barbara summoned George to her office to discuss.

"So, what's the deal with John?" George asked her and Ted as he walked in.

"You know how it is," Ted said. "John has been around a while, he's in charge of Pandora and Icarus, and he does seem to have a say in how things are done around here."

"Tell him I got news for him: not anymore."

"But how? Are you suggesting I go up to him and say, 'Hey, John, guess what—you don't have a say anymore'?"

Jeez, this guy is so naïve that I have to start with the basics. "Set up a series of meetings, with all the top guys in attendance. Leave John out. And make sure he knows he's being left out, okay?"

"I'm with you."

"Then fire a couple of his underlings without consulting

him first. Let John run around a bit figuring out who fired these people. Make it all nebulous. Before you know it, he'll come around."

"That's good, George," Ted said, his swagger rising visibly. "Oh, John will comply or he won't be around much longer."

"He'd better. Otherwise, *you* won't be around much longer."

Ted was clearly taken aback for a moment, but then he laughed. "I hope you're joking."

"I'm not."

Ted looked at Barbara, and she looked away.

Ted's swagger dropped several notches in an instant. He obviously couldn't comprehend what forces were at work. He kept looking at Barbara and George with a blank expression.

"Hey, we're on your side," George said. "Now cut me some costs."

"Thank you, George," Ted said. "I'll take care of John, I promise."

George left the room with exactly what he wanted.

"It doesn't look too good, George," Barbara said. "Cadence Tech backed off from the Pandora deal at the last minute. I'm not sure when Jenner Systems is going to get back to us."

I knew it would come to this. "Well, here's what we can do—"

"Oh, George." Barbara slumped into the chair across from his desk. "When I walked in with the bad news, I was pretty sure you were going to stand up and make that 'I told you so' speech… I appreciate the demeanor, George. You're a good man to have on my side."

Not making a speech has its advantages, Barb. "Ideally, we want to license Pandora to Cadence or Jenner or whoever, even at a steep discount. So tell Ted and his team to keep working at it. But Barb, between you and me, things are in much worse shape. Much worse than what you just told me. So don't be surprised if you see start-up companies across the Valley selling out to the patent sharks a few months down the line."

"My God."

"But that's the worst-case scenario. As for Bodega, we have enough money to hold the fort for a year, and we can always hope things will improve by then. But in the meantime, be prepared for a bloodbath."

With every passing week, more bad news came out of the Valley. The press was all over it again, covering it all on a daily basis, using every metaphor in the book: The dotcom meltdown was a tornado that had shown up from nowhere and destroyed everything in sight; it was a hurricane that had gathered momentum while nobody was paying attention and struck in full force by the time people realized what was going on; it was a tsunami that kept hitting several times in quick succession, with each wave deadlier than the last; and it was a volcanic eruption that had changed the landscape forever.

Every now and then the press ran a story on how even the rich had to get rid of their trappings—a private jet here, a luxury yacht there. Occasionally, the media's "human interest stories" touched on the lesser mortals, too, the real workhorses of the Valley, who had to give up a new car here, take a pay cut there or lose the job altogether.

As the months passed, Barbara became even more deferential to George. She had followed his advice and raised $35 million; they were not in immediate danger of closing. Steve had even made it a habit to occasionally stop by George's office and say hello.

"Vulture investors?" Barbara said to George one day. "The *vulture investors* have started buying up everything in the

Valley? The only investors I ever saw around here were angel investors."

"What's the difference?" George said. "In the evenings I see them all chatting over drinks at my club and I can't tell the angels from the vultures."

"I know, but I'm surprised it all happened in a matter of months."

"Months? Barb, someone can be a big angel investor in Palo Alto this morning *and* the leading vulture investor in Cupertino this afternoon. Why does that surprise you?"

"I know," she said. "So where are we now?"

"I think we did okay. We have a few chinks in the armor, but we haven't lost any vital organs. Not yet anyway."

"You saved us, George. I owe you big time."

"Too soon to say that. I'm still worried about far too many things. Anyway, I'll keep watch, and I'll come to you when I have something to say."

When PANDORA Gave Nothing

SAM OPENED HIS DIARY and started writing. "Six months back, I could do no wrong—no wonder my journal was empty. Now it appears I can do no right—and my diary is overflowing..." He set his journal aside for a moment to collect his thoughts. He thought of calling home, but what was he going to say? *Mom, I don't feel good? Dad, all my work came to nothing?* He was twenty-six years old. Wasn't it a bit too late to call home and cry to Mommy?

He called home. No one answered, and he left a voice mail and lay in bed, trying to clear his thoughts.

"I don't mind telling you," he remembered his father telling him a few years back, "sometimes I look back at my life and realize that nothing much happened to me in a whole decade."

Sam's father came from a family of West Pointers. He and his ex-journalist wife, Jessica, raised Sam near an Army base in Utah. Like all mothers, Jessica told her son he was a smart kid, and for his part, Sam started proving her right by developing a fascination for gee-whiz gadgetry. By the age of 14, he'd started to reverse-engineer some of the tricky things he had seen in movies: telescopes, listening devices, intruder alarms, the works. He started spending all his allowance on electronic components.

"So you want to invent things?" his mother asked him one day.

Nobody had ever asked him that before, but the answer came to him in an instant. "Yes. I want to be an engineer."

As high school graduation approached, Sam was sure his mother would approve of his career choice. She had always encouraged him to read books, figure things out on his own, form his own opinions and defend them—surely she would understand. But he was less sure how his father would react, so Sam asked him straight out, just the way he knew his father liked.

"Dad, are you disappointed that I'm not going to West Point? I mean, I'm not even *trying* to go there."

Sam felt a bit awkward asking it and even more awkward when his father paused to take a good look at him.

"I've been thinking about it a lot, son," he said. "After 'Nam, I haven't fought a single war. All these years I have been spending my time pushing papers and I don't even know why. I don't mind telling you, son, sometimes I look back and realize nothing really happened to me in a whole decade…apart from watching you grow up."

Sam didn't know what to say. He had expected a lecture on how disappointed his father was. He had never imagined his father looked at his own life that way, nor had he expected his father to openly share his feelings. Being treated like a grown-up, more so than his impending graduation, struck Sam as the rite of passage that marked his entry into adulthood.

"So," his father continued, "if you want to follow your heart and do something worthwhile with your life, you get no argument here."

"Yeah, be all you can be, right, Dad?"

"That's my boy." His father gave him a man-hug. "One more thing, Sam: Values are more important than careers. So, Army or no Army, we raised you to be a good man and a leader. Don't you ever forget that."

The phone kept ringing. The caller ID said it was his father.

"Hey, Junior Ranger, what's going on with you? Staying out of trouble?"

"Dad, there's no way I can stay out of *this* trouble."

"Son, you want to change the world," his father said. "With a goal like that, there's got to be a setback or two."

"But it's different when you live here and face it every day. I mean, you didn't go through anything like this when you were my age."

His father was silent.

"Sorry, Dad," Sam said. "I didn't mean that. I meant to say there was no *uncertainty* in your career. You always had—always have—your job."

"It's okay, son, I'm old enough to take that. You're right—I never had to doubt if I was going to keep my job the next day. But I spent a good three years of my life wondering if I was going to remain alive for the next hour. That kinda evens it out, don't you think?"

"Sorry, Dad. I guess I have it better than you did."

"Son, the question isn't who has it better. The question is whether you realize what a blessing it is to be in your position."

"Blessing?" Sam said. "How's *this* a blessing?"

"There comes a time in everyone's life—and I do mean in *everyone's* life—when you ask yourself what it is that you've been doing with your life. Sometimes you even realize that whatever you've been doing all your life, you've been doing it wrong. Dead wrong… Son, you want that realization to hit you when you're 70? Or 50? Or when you're still young, with your whole life still ahead of you?"

Sam couldn't think of anything to say. His head was spinning.

"Are you there, son?"

"Yes, Dad."

"You just have to begin a new chapter. No, no, make that a new book. What the heck, just leave the Valley if that's what it takes to get you a new start."

"No, I'll stay here to see what's next. I still have a job."

"See, you still have a job. So it isn't so bad, is it? In any case, let me offer you one last piece of advice. Things can change pretty fast in your situation. And when it happens, don't sit on the sidelines and watch the show. Seize the moment, son, seize the moment."

An Honorable Failure

SAM OFTEN WONDERED why he and his team were still around. Barbara had asked him to wrap up the work as soon as possible and complete the documentation. Why she didn't scrap Pandora altogether, particularly when all the clients and leads had disappeared practically overnight, was beyond Sam. But it wasn't something he could ask anyone about. *Barb, how come my project is still around?* No, he definitely wasn't going to ask her that.

While the work went on, the change of attitude toward the geeks became more blatant by the day. The top guys and even the middle managers no longer "discussed the requirements with the architects" but simply "talked to the techies." They no longer "wondered if development had the bandwidth to accommodate the new dates" but simply "made it clear that the new deadlines must be met."

They routinely "talked to the developers about the big-picture issues and put things into perspective"—something they hadn't dared to do six months earlier. They no longer got excited about "our guys cutting their teeth on the new technologies" but simply "expected the employees to brush up on whatever it is that they're working on these days."

Sam walked past the rows of cubes, noting how quiet the office had become. It wasn't just that Bodega now employed fewer people—the people had become a lot quieter.

But in his aisle, things were a tad chirpier. He approached Vick and Jennifer to see what it was all about.

"What are we, horrible or honorable?" Jennifer was asking Vick.

"Still running the numbers. Just a moment," Vick said. "We're trying to figure out if investing in Bodega was better than—are you ready for this?—drinking beer."

"Beer?"

"Yes, beer." Vick told him that when it came to evaluating how a given company fared in the new economy, there was no better benchmark than beer. A bottle of beer cost a dollar on average, and once it was consumed, the empty bottle could be redeemed for ten cents. "So you invest a dollar in beer, you have a good time drinking it and in the end you're left with ten cents. A bad investment."

"That's an expense, not an investment," Sam said. "But I see your point. I practically lost all my money. I think I'm left with fifteen cents on every dollar I invested. So I fared better than beer?"

"Congrats!"

"Did you figure all this out?" Sam asked.

"Oh, it wasn't me," Vick said. "I don't know who came up with this measure, but it's quite new paradigm all over the Valley."

"And by no means is it the only measure," Jennifer said. "So much money was lost that some people I know have started measuring the declines on a *log* scale, as in 'My net worth is down three decibels this month.'"

"Ha-ha."

After a few more minutes of computing, Vick declared: "Bodega fared better than beer. *We beat beer.* Come on, guys, we should celebrate!"

"Sure, what do you have in mind?" Sam said. "Oh, wait—I know."

"Yes, beer it is," Vick said. "No, we're not getting drunk, my friend. Not anymore. We're reviewing our investments and pursuing a prudent diversification strategy."

"It makes an interesting tag line, don't you think?" Jennifer said. "'Bodega InfoTech… Better Than Beer.' Maybe we should put that on our website, on the Investor Relations page."

Mystery House

As he drove around Winchester Boulevard for no reason other than to clear his mind, Sam kept thinking about Kelly. After a couple of unsuccessful attempts to get through to her, he had stopped trying for fear of coming across as a stalker. And in the aftermath of the dotcom bust, he didn't even *want* to date anyone for a while.

As he neared the entry ramp to Interstate 280, there it was, the Mystery House. According to the local press, it was the most popular landmark in the San Jose area, and according to many it was the only landmark. In any case, by way of an updated Mark Twainian truth, it was a building that everyone wanted to see but no one got around to see. Having nothing better to do, Sam parked his car and went in.

It was a large house on four acres of prime real estate comprised of 160 rooms and six kitchens. According to the brochure the cashier had given him, it had taken many years and millions of dollars to build the house, but—perhaps this was the mystery part—there had never been a basic building plan on which to base the construction.

As Sam walked through the house, he began to see the results of not having a plan. There were many doors in the floor, passages that led nowhere, stairs that went straight to the ceiling, and far too many things that served no purpose, all befitting a mystery house.

But that wasn't half the mystery, as it turned out. The real mystery surrounded Sarah Winchester, who had owned the house and paid for its numerous renovations and reconstructions. She had spent millions specifically to ensure that something or other was always being repaired or renovated or reconstructed, mostly for no purpose and all too often flying in the face of reason.

But even *that* wasn't the weirdest part. Claiming that distinction was the fact that Sarah had spent all those millions just because the ghost of her dead husband had told her in a dream that she would be safe from evil spirits as long as she was renovating or repairing the house.

That was it—there was never a reason, much less a plan. Day in, day out, the house stood witness to round-the-clock activity with no purpose. Year in, year out, everyone created work for everybody else and no one asked any questions.

Sam had set out that afternoon to clear his mind, but he returned more disturbed than ever. He opened his journal and started writing:

> With the turn of the century, the Mystery House finally acquired a purpose… In fact, if I were somebody big and powerful, such as the CEO of a new-economy company, I would require all my employees to take a mandatory tour of the Mystery House every year. True to the rumors, the ghost of Winchester is very much alive, and it's trying to tell us something…

✳✳✳

"Cheer up, Sam," Kris said. "You're at work. You aren't paid to have these thoughts."

Sam looked up and smiled. "I don't know how you can be so upbeat."

"That's easy. My life revolves around two things, and those two things haven't changed."

"What things?"

"My visa. It was valid then and it's valid now."

"And the other?"

"The office coffee. It was horrible then, it's horrible now."

"That's it?"

"I was just joking. Of course there's more. Let's go get a coffee and I'll tell you the story of my life."

Sam shook his head.

Kris looked at him. "Okay then, I'll leave you alone."

After Kris had left, Sam kept thinking about the Mystery House. *All along, I toiled on Pandora because I thought I was changing the world. If only I'd asked some basic, fundamental questions...but* what *questions?*

Sam couldn't face work anymore. As he walked out, he passed George, and for a moment he thought George was giving him a dirty look. *This is odd. It's not like we ever spoke to each other.* Sam kept walking toward the exit. When he opened the door, he saw George walking a few paces behind him. He held the door open, and George walked out without saying the customary thanks or even nodding.

What's up with this guy? Sam walked toward his car, not looking in George's direction again. *But then, he was never the friendly type to begin with. At least Barbara still says hello when she sees me, so I have that going for me.*

He paused. Come to think of it, when she said hello, it was no longer the old "I'm so glad we have you on our team" hello.

It was a wary hello, more like a "I'm making an effort to be nice, so please walk away before I change my mind" hello.

Into the wee hours that night, Sam lay in bed wondering what was going on.

Pandora has found no customers, not a single line of my code has been deployed in the real world, Barbara is distancing herself and George probably has something against me. Somehow I still have a job at 640 San Bernardino Avenue. If only there was a tour guide to explain this *mystery house to me.*

Seizing the Moment

SAM GLANCED AT THE ODOMETER as he cruised along northbound I-280. About twenty miles to go. It was a Saturday morning, and he had planned to drive up to Woodside and then ride his bicycle to La Honda. Cycling on that tree-lined stretch of California 84 always offered him a bit more than the usual health benefits: it cleared his mind when it was too full; and it inspired new thoughts when it was too empty.

He kept thinking of Pandora. The project had been pretty much all wrapped up, but it had never found any customers—did that mean he and the rest of the team were going to lose their jobs? Losing the job was superficial compared with the real issue: what was next? What was he going to do with his life? "Seize the moment," his father had told him, but what moment he was going to seize?

An angry honk from behind broke his chain of thought.

Damn. Gotta be more alert when driving.

While lost in his thoughts, he had taken the Saratoga Avenue exit, the exit that led him to Bodega on weekdays. He cursed how the mind works, with some references to Pavlov's dog and soon merged with the traffic on Saratoga Avenue. He kept looking for a gap in the oncoming traffic so he could take a take a U-turn and get back on the interstate. Then he saw Java Junkies.

Might as well get a coffee. He pulled into the parking lot and got out. He stood there for a few minutes, taking in the crisp morning air and trying to clear his mind.

Java Junkies was the same as ever, with the familiar inviting aroma of medium-roast coffee and the usual Saturday morning demographic of older people returning from their morning walks with newspapers in hand and young people venturing out with some gadget or other in hand. Months after the new economy had collapsed, the old economy—the coffee shop, the diner next door, the laundromat around the corner—stood proud and happy.

For a moment, Sam considered owning a coffee shop or a restaurant or a bakery where nothing much happened, ever. Then it took him all of ten seconds to think better of it—he'd be bored to death within days.

As he watched happy face after happy face leave Java Junkies just as he had seen on many a morning, a back-to-basics realization shook him to the core—not because it was profound or life-changing but because it was laughably simple and painfully obvious. Indeed, that was the problem with any of the "simple truths" in the world of business—in the end, it always took a gaggle of complete idiots or a team of all-knowing geniuses to overlook them.

Deliver something of value to a lot of people and keep them happy; when they keep coming back for more, you'll have a good thing going.

Everything that Bodega ever did was based on the assumption that a handful of big corporations were going to license the "world-changing technologies" that it produced. In the end, all it ever took to bring everything down was for that one assumption to go wrong, which it did. But what if Bodega catered to thousands of happy *individual* customers instead of a few faceless corporations? And what if those individuals kept coming back, as was obviously the case with Java Junkies? Did *he* have any ideas involving cool technology that could deliver something of value to the common man?

God, I've been chasing data transfers and system integration and test scripts and documentation and project audits, thinking I was changing the world. But I had the real thing right under my nose all the time.

He trashed all his plans for the day. Instead, he would go home and resume his work on the cell phone prototype. Or anything from his PWD that offered a real benefit to a real customer. Once he had something ready—in two weeks at most—he was going to talk to Barbara.

His mind kept racing. Given the state of dotcom, what was Barbara going to say? What if she liked the idea but had no money to fund it? It wasn't going to be easy, but he was going to do whatever it took to see it through. Yes, he was going to seize the moment and help Bodega make a comeback. Help Bodega? No, it was way more than that. It was his chance—perhaps his real chance—to change the world.

Sam didn't even want the coffee anymore. He wanted to go home and resume work, starting with the flowcharts. He turned abruptly to return to his car and almost bumped into someone.

"I'm so sorry," he said, walking away. "I should've seen you coming."

"Yes," she said, "then you might even have recognized me."

Sam turned and looked at her, still a bit flustered. It was Kelly, of all people. But she wasn't at all like he had remembered her. She was wearing a business suit and a modest blue shirt, she held an empty flask in one hand and an attaché case in the other, and she had a harried look befitting someone who was about to face a long day at work.

"Kelly," he managed to say, "it's nice to see you."

"Sam, it's nice to be recognized."

"Well, I…"

She laughed. "Just messing with you. So how are you?"

"Good." *No, I don't feel good. I have a job, but I don't know how long it'll last. I got a great idea today, but I don't know how to follow it through. I run into you after all these months and I don't know what to say. My best option is to say something nice and slip away.* "Sorry. I mean—"

"There's a lot that both of us could be sorry about, but I'm not going there. Things happen."

"So," he said, breathing a little easier, "what's with the suit?" As her eyebrows rose, he hastily added, "I mean, on a Saturday."

"That's okay, Sam. Party girls need a job, too. And sometimes it means meeting clients on a Saturday."

Sam wanted to slip away, but there was something in her demeanor that made him feel welcome to stay on. He looked at her. "And what do you do?"

"Loan approver." She didn't sound too happy. "I work in real estate."

Funny how many people turn gloomy at the mere mention of work. "You like it?"

She was about to say something but hesitated. "Oh no," she finally said, "I shouldn't really be boring you with my problems. Well… I should be going."

Seize the moment, Sam. "I know it might be a bit awkward, but…"

"Yes?"

"Well… I just wanted to say you can tell me what's on your

mind. I mean, we're talking *work*, right? Don't worry, your secrets will be safe with me."

"I said it was boring. I didn't say it was a secret. But if you really want to know, my life is reduced to attending meetings all day long, with no time at all for real work."

"You work at *my* office?"

She sniggered a little and shook her head. "No real work, and nothing much happens, ever. They want you to be a 'team player,' so in the end no one takes the 'risk' of saying anything new or even interesting."

"Ah, you work with grown-ups?"

She started to lighten up. "Jeez, look at you. You're so cheerful and nice to everyone you run into, even to someone who dumped you over a phone call."

"Hey no problem," Sam said, trying hard to keep an even tone. "I kinda deserved it, you know."

"So tell me, have you become 'all grown-up' or are you still dreaming big?"

"If I answer that question, I run the risk of saying something new and interesting."

Kelly laughed, if only just a little. Then she did something he hadn't expected: She looked into his eyes and held his gaze.

Sam stood transfixed, wondering if he should ask her the question. But how? Could he ask her just like that, out in the open? What if she was seeing someone? On the other hand, what was the harm in asking? Wait—what if he ended up coming across as a jerk?

Then *she* asked *him* the question. "So, you want to go in and grab a coffee and tell me all about your dreams? I'm sure it will be a refreshing change from anything else I hear these days."

Sam looked at her in disbelief. Yes, it was the same Kelly who had once told him he was "such a nice guy."

"I'd love to talk," he said. "I really need someone to talk to, and like I said on our first date, you're the smartest girl I've ever met."

"*Liar.*"

STRATEGY MEETS COMMON SENSE

GEORGE DIDN'T LIKE WHAT HE SAW. The meeting invite from Steve's personal secretary said "Review of Strategy and Operations." That was it, no details. He suspected the agenda was being kept vague on purpose. Perhaps they were going to discuss a key new initiative or a possible merger with another ailing dotcom or a complete reorg of Bodega. Or—who knew?—there was also the possibility that Steve was going to congratulate his management team for ensuring the survival of Bodega through the dotcom bust.

The phone rang. It was Barbara. "I need to pick your brain," she said. "Can we meet at the club this evening and discuss a few strategic issues?"

Specifically what? George remained silent, waiting for Barbara to resume.

"We're trying to answer a question that Steve asked me yesterday: Where do we go from here?"

Back to business school, Barb. That's where you've got to go and learn the basics all over. "Sure," he said, "that's an interesting question, and I'll give it some thought."

***

George sipped his single malt and looked at Barbara. "Tell me again what it is we do," he said.

"What do you mean? We develop software, right?"

No, Barb. We employ a bunch of nerds in the hope that the rest of the nerds out there are going to buy what our nerds produce. Oh, because we're a "new economy" company, we hang up posters all over the place full of words like panacea, nirvana *and* karma. *And because we're "changing the world," we party all the time like a rock star's entourage cut loose on Las Vegas.*

"George?"

"I don't think there is anything fundamentally wrong with what we do," George said. "This place could use more structure and control. That's all I can think at the moment."

"More structure?"

"And control. We once had truckloads of cash and we spent it all on useless things. We've really got to establish centralized control over cash."

"But, George, I don't think Steve is going to care for the structures-and-controls bit. You got anything *strategic?*"

Ah, you need a talking point. Okay, I'll give you one. "In my experience, most of the time these 'strategic' matters come down to common sense. So I'll ask you a simple question and leave it at that."

"I can't wait."

"Okay, here we go. The man on the street benefits from what Bodega does because…" He paused for effect. "Now, Barb, complete that sentence in twenty words or less. When you have a clear and simple answer to that, you'll know you have a good thing going. Or even a game changer."

"George! By that yardstick, practically every company in the Valley is a complete failure."

"I'm shocked!" George said, raising his glass.

***

"I love it," Steve said. "That's a very good question to ask. So, do we have anything that stands up to Barbara's litmus test?"

Yeah, Barbara's litmus test. George didn't mind Barbara's publicly taking credit for his ideas as long as she made sure he was rewarded later with a generous bonus or a pay hike. Indeed, that was what Barbara had always done, since their days at Interstate.

"We have a few proposals," Ted said. "There's a really good one from the Sedona guys. I'll let Eric speak for it."

Eric rose and walked to the head of the table. "I'll keep it brief," he said. "We need a product that helps people to do day-to-day things. It's common sense, really: Put yourself in the shoes of the average Joe and make his life simple. Hotel reservations, car rentals, cruises, merchandise—"

"Aren't we late to enter those markets?" Steve said. "People are already doing all that online."

"But they hardly buy any *groceries*," Eric said. "Think about it. It handily passes Barbara's test, if we pull it off quickly we'll be the first to do it, and it has tremendous future potential— once you start selling groceries, you can leverage it to sell many other things."

"Groceries, huh?" Steve said. "That changes us from a technology company to a consumer company... That's quite a change!"

"Of course," Ted said. "We've got to fundamentally rethink our business. But then, that's what this meeting is all about."

"Have you discussed any of this with the techies?"

"Oh, no," Ted said, shaking his head. "You know how it is. They're way too absorbed in the little details to grasp anything strategic."

"So what's the plan?"

"Once you approve this, we'll engage the techies at the appropriate level."

"Okay then," Steve said, "I like the idea, and it does offer a tangible benefit to the customer, and that's never a bad thing. Above all, I trust you guys and I'm sure you'll see it through. Barb, if the numbers look okay to you, please approve the funding. Ted, I want you to take New Horizons to everyone at Bodega, pronto."

Then he got up and left.

As Ted and Eric kept talking, George tuned out of the meeting to collect his thoughts. After a few minutes, he, too, got up and left.

George couldn't believe his ears. *No bonus?* He looked back at Barbara. She was apologetic as hell, but that was of no comfort.

"This isn't how it's supposed to work," he said.

"I know, George, but what do you expect? Bodega has no money to pay bonuses. *To anyone.*"

"Not even to the man who saved this company from oblivion? Barb, Bodega is still in business because *I* told you to raise cash. *I* was the sole person to give you sane advice at a time when every Internet fanboy here was partying like there was no tomorrow. Now you tell me that *I* don't matter one bit?"

"Oh, George, of course you matter. I value your expertise more than ever. And Steve likes you, too."

"I didn't sign up here to be *liked* by somebody."

"I know you're upset, but you've got to trust me on this… George?"

"Yes?"

"You look really upset. Don't you trust me?"

"Of course I do."

"I'll take care of your bonus when the finances improve, I promise."

That's if *the finances improve, Barb.* "Glad to hear it."

New Horizons

"New Horizons," it said on the screen. And it had an italicized subtitle to boot: "Selling groceries from an Internet-enabled cell phone."

Sam could practically feel his heart pounding against his rib cage. *He* could have been the one making that presentation if only he had wrapped up the design and taken it to Barbara a week sooner. And yes, like Vick had said a few minutes ago without actually meaning it, his whole life could very well revolve around it in the months and years to come.

"Look around the Valley, guys," Ted began the meeting. "Far too many businesses have folded. But some have survived. Exactly which ones, you ask? The kind that deliver something of v-a-l-u-e to the customer." He continued for many minutes on the same theme, making the usual power gestures with his hands. "To sum up," he finally said, "we've got to deliver v-a-l-u-e. Now I hand it over to Eric. He'll walk you through the details."

Great. Now that you're out of your depth, you hand it over to an underling. No wonder you're in management.

"Let's begin with a simple question," Eric said. "Who among us really *loves* doing the milk runs?" Having asked what he must have thought was a great opening question, he waited for several seconds for the obvious answer.

A voice from the back provided the expected answer. "Not many, I guess."

"Exactly," Eric said. "What if we develop the technology to do it online? Imagine a world where people can buy groceries on the Internet. Oh, wait—it gets better. What if people can buy groceries from their *cell phones?*"

Where did you get this idea?

"Whoa," John said. "Don't you think that's a pretty complicated thing for a *phone* to do?"

"Of course, we're talking about an advanced phone. We've been talking to some guys in telecom, and what we've seen so far is quite promising."

Oh, why didn't I talk to someone in telecom?

"Okay, let's play along for a moment with your soon-to-be-invented gadget," John said. "So the customer places the order by typing it all out on his cell phone. Have you thought about the delivery address?"

"Huh?"

"Do you really expect the consumer to *type in* the delivery address on a small handheld device? Bad idea. You're looking at a ton of typos."

"Of course, we have to work out these details," Eric said, clearly ill at ease. "Trust me, if that's ever a problem, we have a backup plan."

"Whoa," John said with a sideways glance at Ted, "this is our first meeting on this topic and you're already on to your *backup* plan. Something tells me that the backup plan will soon be the de facto plan, which is to say you really don't have much of a plan to begin with."

Eric was visibly taken aback at how John was coming down on him. He looked at Ted.

"Look," Ted said to John, "let him explain the idea, all right? You can shoot him down later."

"I'm not shooting down anyone here," John said. "Just asking for specifics. I'm not about to go back to my team and talk about some pie-in-the-sky idea. I need *specifics*."

"Oh great," Ted said. "You just called it a pie-in-the-sky idea, even before we're done presenting it. If *that* isn't shooting it down, what is?"

"Let me say this again. I was just asking for specifics. *You're* the one who started it by claiming I'm trying to shoot this down—"

"Enough!" Ted snapped. "Let's get back to the meeting, okay?"

Seize the moment, Sam. "Actually, what John described— the delivery address—won't be a problem."

Everyone in the room looked at Sam.

"It won't?" John asked.

"The service provider will have the customer's address stored in his database. Also, it should be part of the customer sign-up process."

"I appreciate it, Sam," Ted said. "It's good to have people who *solve* problems on our team instead of just complaining."

John gave Ted a nasty look and then turned toward Sam. "I get it, Sam, but how is this all going to work together? Don't you see several pieces missing in action?"

Sam looked at Eric as if to say, "May I?" Eric nodded, looking pleasantly surprised and obviously encouraged at how quickly Sam was grasping *his* idea.

So he didn't steal it. It probably occurred to him just like it occurred to me. And he wrapped up his work a week before I did and so there he is. "The solution lies in middleware." Sam paused for a moment and looked around the meeting room. "Guess what—we can reuse a lot of the Pandora stuff."

"Ah," Eric said, "you are the lead architect on Pandora. Obviously you can see where we're going with this." Ted, who had been looking at Sam blank-faced, nodded wisely as if his world had suddenly started making sense again.

No, Eric, there's so much going on that I don't know where to start.

John turned toward Eric. "Not to rain on the parade, but the idea is a bit far-fetched. Are you really sure it's all going to work?"

Sam hesitated, wondering if he should intervene again. In any case, it looked like John was making an observation and not really asking a question.

Eric spoke before Sam could say anything. "Come on, John, barely four years back, the Internet itself was a far-fetched idea. Who would have thought we could book a flight from the comfort of our homes?" Then he looked at Sam as if to say, "Am I right?"

John shook his head and remained silent.

Sam kept playing John's words in his mind. *What's going on with John? This isn't like him at all.*

As the questions petered out, Eric went back to the slides, his confidence growing slide by slide. He started sharing more details: the system design, the data flows, the logistics and so on. He paused regularly to ask if there were any questions or comments, often looking in Sam's direction.

The first few slides were a little sketchy for Sam's taste. Eric's strength was mostly on the business side, after all. But to be fair, he was doing a decent job of communicating the concept in general. As the slides continued, though, Sam cringed—all in all, it was more or less what he would have designed.

Two things you must do when you have a new idea: Prepare a business plan and engage the top guys early on. I failed on both counts. Now it's Eric's idea.

"Okay," John said, "so what's our mechanism to communicate with the vendors?"

"Well, like I said, it's too early in the game," Eric said. "We can discuss the details in due course."

"Oh, there you go again! On one hand, you come to us with a new idea saying it's the next big thing, but on the other hand, I hate to leave a meeting without having heard *a single actionable item.* I don't even know who I should be putting on this project. I mean, shouldn't you guys have engaged me sooner on this?"

Eric and Ted looked at each other blankly for a few seconds. Then they did something that Sam wouldn't have expected them to do: They both looked at him as if to say, "Can you help?"

"Well," Sam said, "when it comes to the mechanism that John was asking about, there are three ways to do it. We can send two or three batch files a day to the grocers. Or there can be a set of text files on the grocers' sales order database that we could append in real time. Or we can post XML docs at a predefined http location that the grocers can download and parse."

Eric and Ted looked at him in disbelief.

"You're good, Sam," Ted said. "Really good."

Eric then presented the rest of the slides, which focused on the timeline, resources and project communications. The meeting degenerated into the usual post-meeting din, centering mostly on everyday words such as *buy, sell, store, shop* and *bill*—but appended with the magical prefix *e*.

In a while, everyone started to troop out.

Eric smiled as Sam approached him. "Thanks, man," Eric said.

"No problem."

"So," Eric said, "looks like we had an interesting meeting, huh?"

Sam remained silent. He really wanted to know what was going on with John, but he wasn't sure what to ask Eric, let alone *if* he should be asking Eric.

"Just between us," Eric said, looking around to make sure he wasn't within anyone else's earshot, "John has been trying to kill this project."

Why would he do that? What's going on around here?

"It's a personal thing between Ted and John," Eric continued. "From what I hear, it's been going on for a long time."

Sam tried to find something safe to say. "I've got a few more ideas. What's a good time to discuss?"

"Ted and I have to meet Barbara now. Let's meet first thing tomorrow morning if you're free."

Second Chance

"So what do you make of this next big thing?" Sam asked Vick once they'd gotten back to their desks after the New Horizons meeting.

"So what do you make of the politics?" Vick said.

"I'll tell you all about that sideshow, but not now. I've got to meet with Barb in a few minutes."

"Sideshow? Politics was the *whole* show. Come on, dude, it was all playing out there in full high-def with Dolby digital surround sound. Did you fall asleep or what? I thought you were wide awake, the way you kept answering the questions. Good job, by the way."

"So in the end, what's your take?" Sam said. "I mean, on New Horizons."

"I've seen this movie before and I know how it ends."

"Really?"

"Why not?" Vick said. "Pandora was just like this. We all gave it our hundred percent and then some. And then it came to nothing. And you know what? That was without the politics."

"I know, but I think this one is going to be different."

"Do you want to tell me why?"

Sam took a deep breath. "Because it makes sense. Remember, this has always been my idea. I once even asked you to work with me on this."

"Doesn't ring a bell. When was that?"

"Never mind." Sam opened his laptop and showed Vick his "PWD" folder.

Vick looked at the folder for a few seconds in obvious disbelief. "Database design… validation logic… storefront… payment methods. Dude, you've obviously put in a lot of work. Too bad, but it's Eric's project now."

"I've been thinking about it all through the meeting," Sam said. "To be fair, I don't think I ever discussed it with Eric, so it's not like he stole it from me. In fact, I approached him, and he was totally open to working with me."

"And why shouldn't he? You'll do the real work and he gets the credit. And if it fails, it'll be your fault. Not a bad deal for him, is it?"

"Do you really see him that way?"

"I see *all of them* that way," Vick said. "They all want to hog the credit. And if they believe they won't get the credit, they want to shoot it down. *That's* what's going on with John, if you ask me. For two years he was such an angel because he got a ton of credit for all the progress while the likes of you and me did the real work. Now that he isn't getting any credit, he's showing his true colors."

That's it? Or is there more to John's departure?

"Eric and Ted *will* hog the credit," Vick continued. "If they approve the funding, of course. If it gets deployed. If it works."

"Oh, it'll work," Sam said. "I'm telling you it will."

"I wasn't so sure. Now that you've weighed in, I guess it's all settled."

"Seriously, all our hard work on Pandora came to nothing. What do we have going for us now? This cool project. *And we can leverage everything we did on Pandora. What's not to like?*"

"So what's the plan?"

"I'll show Barb what I've got here so she knows it's my idea, too."

"Careful, that could mean even more office politics."

"No, man, I won't go after Eric or anyone. I'll just focus on what I bring to the table. I'll stay positive on this."

"Oh, like you know how to go negative."

Sam shrugged and looked at his watch. Two minutes to 5. He headed upstairs to Barbara's office armed with his laptop.

"Ted told me what I already knew," Barbara said. "You'll make a good development manager."

Development manager? But… that's John's job.

"I just approved the funding for New Horizons," Barbara continued. "Eric has some really cool ideas, but you know his expertise is mainly on the business side. We need someone on the technical side, someone really smart and diligent to see it through."

Eric's idea? Wait till I show you what I got.

"Of course you're excited, I can see that. Oh, there's just one thing that worries me, Sam. Let me get it off my chest."

"What is it?"

"On a critical project like this, there'll be enough credit to go around. We're all on the same side, Sam. We don't want people to fight over little things."

"Why are you telling me this, Barb? This is how I work anyway."

"Because that's what happened with John and Ted. They could both take credit for what they brought to the table, you know. But they kept fighting over who was more valuable to Bodega. In the end, one of them had to be shown the door."

My God. John is out?

"Look, now we have you on the technical side and Eric on the business side. I don't ever want to see you two bickering over who gets the credit for what. In fact, that's one reason I think of *you* as the right man for the job. Sam, can I count on you to stay above these petty office politics?"

"Of course," Sam said almost intuitively. *Oh, wait—does that mean...* He remained silent, wondering what to say. *Am I going to tell her the truth and start this project on a sour note, or am I going to give up a good chunk of the credit for the chance—my real chance—to change the world?*

"Good," Barbara said. "You need anything?"

Sam nodded.

"Don't hesitate to ask." She looked at him pleasantly. "What is it?"

"I get to pick my team."

Boot Camp

In many ways, George's education began not when he
enrolled in business school but a few years after he had gradu-
ated, when Interstate Logistics had three bad quarters in a row.
George would always remember that morning. He'd poured
himself some coffee and opened his front door to pick up the
newspaper when he saw the headline: "Leadership change at
Interstate Logistics." The board had fired the CEO and announced
that it was hiring a new guy to "bring a fresh perspective to its
operations."

*Funny, I thought I was a senior guy around here, and this is
how they tell me what's going on.*

But as it turned out, reporting to a new guy had its advantages. It allowed his boss, Barbara, to dust off an old plan
of hers and present it to someone who hadn't seen it before.
She had presented the idea to the old guys in different flavors
and under various fancy names, but it had all fallen on deaf
ears. Now seeing her chance, Barbara polished the numbers
a bit and gave it a yet another new name: Eureka Initiative.
Whereas the old guys had understood the details and rejected
the proposal because it carried high risk, the new guy didn't

care for the details but approved the plan anyway *because* it sounded risky. He had signed up to "take risks," and there was his chance to do just that.

Those days, Interstate had about a hundred warehouses across America to support its distribution business. Barbara's idea, in a nutshell, was to close most of the warehouses and keep everything centralized at six warehouses. It could bring in higher profits—if it worked.

Barbara was given the money she needed, but on the promise that she showed results in nine months. She got things rolling right away, with her right-hand man George in tow.

George had always held the view that what the public knew about any company was at best a series of shows: press releases, CEO interviews, commercials, financial results, earnings conferences and other lies. The real success or failure of any firm was determined by how it managed its precious resources, the most important of which was invariably the cash.

While the aggressive, outgoing Barbara flew around the country to oversee the reorganization and to seek new contracts, George chose to remain at base camp, tracking numbers and coordinating activities, often telling Barbara where to go and what to do.

It worked well. After about seven months, they started to feel an undercurrent of success. Interstate's customers were becoming more receptive, the truckers were becoming more responsive and the delivery lead times were getting shorter and shorter. It was all starting to come together, at least as George and Barbara saw it.

"The Board isn't buying it, George," Barbara told him. "I keep telling them we're getting there. But they want to see results."

"Tell them we feel it on the shop floor and we feel it when we talk to the customers," George said. "It will take a few months for the numbers to show it."

"They aren't willing to listen. They don't even want to look like they might be willing to listen. That's because *the street* isn't willing to listen. They want to be able to go to Wall Street and say, 'At last, here are the results,' or else."

"Else what?"

"They'll fire the CEO one of these days and get a new one. And it could get much worse."

"Worse?"

"From what I hear," Barbara said, "they could kill Eureka and blame *us* for misleading the new CEO."

"What?"

"I know. I feel sick just thinking about it, George. Not fair. Not fair at all."

George shook his head. Fair or not, he knew Barbara was stating a simple truth: When things went well, the CEO types took credit for the success, and when things didn't go well, they fired a lot of people and took credit for making "bold and risky decisions." Taking responsibility for failures wasn't part of their job description.

"You know," George said, "sometimes I think they all live in a fantasy world."

"True. They believe that if they keep beating us up, we'll magically deliver an impressive turnaround in *two months*. How's that even possible?"

After Barbara left, George pondered what his "results-driven" buddies from business school would do in his situation. He knew the law allowed some flexibility in reporting the financial results; he knew that on any given morning, corporate America interpreted the law in the way that would suit it best that afternoon;

and he even knew that many of his buddies window-dressed the results every September, year after year, like clockwork. In fact, some of them were brash enough to tell George that when it came to truth, financial results were up there with press releases—avoid stating anything demonstrably false and you could get away with a lot of things.

As the clock kept ticking, George found himself fantasizing about how, if he really wanted to, he could fix the numbers through the usual tricks of the trade. Soon he started redoing the numbers if only to see how far he could go in that hypothetical situation. As the gap between the "desired" results and the "actual" results kept narrowing, it all became less of a fantasy and more of a plan, often venturing into the gray areas of accounting and occasionally going beyond the law.

In the days that followed, George looked for opportunities everywhere. He over-reported the revenues, recognized the revenues earlier than usual, deferred some expenses to a later period, underestimated the bad debts, window-dressed the receivables, altered the inventory valuations—all the gray-area accounting digressions he could think of. The numbers started to look better but fell just short of the "ideal" numbers.

Having exhausted all the ideas, George needed one last trick to tide him over. He started working his way through his rolodex to see if any of his buddies could help.

"George! Always a pleasure," Clara said as she shook hands with George. Next to her was her right-hand man, Tom.

"Well, there is some business, too," George said as he sat down. "I have a huge favor to ask. Can you call Joel and help me secure some new business from Wonderworld? Not for me but for Interstate."

"Really, George, 'not for me but for Interstate'? Tell me what's in it for you."

"Well, there's something for *you* as well. So you help me out and I'll return the favor."

"How?"

"Look, Interstate is *this* close to a turnaround. If you want to make a killing on the stock, this is the time to get in. When the results come out next month, you'll know what I mean."

"Hmm, that's good to know," Clara said. "So, nobody knows you're here, right?"

"Don't worry," George said. He had let Barbara in on some of his accounting changes, but this meeting with Clara was too sensitive to let anybody in on. "But as it stands now, we might miss our EPS target narrowly. And you know how the market reacts—you miss the target by half a cent and they downgrade you to junk. On the other hand, you beat the street by the same half a cent and they all go gaga. They've completely lost their sense of judgment."

"So?"

"So you'll help me in getting the new business from Wonderworld. That'll help me beat the street. And when it does, you'll make a killing on the stock. Make sense?"

"Yes, it does, except I don't see what's in it for Joel. Why would he do something that may not be in Wonderworld's interests?"

"That's where you come in," George said. "Since you'll make a killing, when the time comes, you'll do Joel a good turn. Tell him you'll cut him a sweet deal sometime and that should persuade him to help me now. I'm sure we can work this out as we go along."

"Let me think it over," Clara said. "If anything is needed from your side, Tom will call you."

George had met Tom before, but he had never dealt with him directly. He looked at him skeptically.

"Believe me, he's good," Clara said. "So, sounds like we have a plan, huh?"

"I'll drink to that," George said and raised his whiskey for the first time during the meeting. He needed that drink for sure. In one short day, he'd committed more crimes than in the last five years put together. But then, like Clara had told him way back in business school, if one were to do dirty business at all, one had to be quick and efficient about it.

"Calculated risks pay off at Interstate," the newspapers said and went on to praise the CEO for "making bold moves, engineering an impressive turnaround and delivering the results on a tight timeline." What's more, the future was brighter than ever, with the company securing promising contracts from industry giants like Wonderworld.

The board members were delirious, having driven the "decisive management change" that had led to the results. Some of them were even interviewed on TV, where they proudly explained how they all did their jobs as the well-meaning custodians of the shareholder wealth. Giving credit where it was due, the board promoted Barbara to senior vice president.

While Barbara got all the credit, she made sure that George received a substantial bonus, larger than what she had received herself, in fact. The gesture wasn't lost on George—it more or less established the ground rules of their relationship for years to come.

As months went by, things got better and better for Interstate. They got rid of the remaining superfluous warehouses, completed the streamlining of trucking operations, signed on a few new accounts and started delivering results. Only this time, the numbers were real.

George was at again, rolling back the inventory valuations, changing all the revenue and expense numbers and generally undoing all the sly things he had done in the previous quarters.

He was smart and careful about it all. He did not undo everything in one quarter—that wouldn't escape the eyes of a shrewd auditor. Instead, he did it over three quarters. Throughout those months, he kept his own set of secret books with all the adjustments and counter-adjustments and carefully tracked every dollar that was ever cooked up. On the side, he made sure that Clara made money just as he had promised and that Joel of Wonderworld had received his kickback just as he had requested.

It was a frightening undertaking, but he pulled it off carefully. In the end, Interstate had absorbed all the overstated profits and still shown decent profits for three quarters in a row. Most important for George, he came out clean.

For George and Barbara, it was the scariest time of their lives, but they learned their lessons. George learned that nothing was illegal so long as you corrected it before the SEC caught it. Barbara seemed to have learned one thing: stick to the front office and leave the numbers to George.

And they never looked back.

Master Plan

After tucking his children into bed, George went to his study and poured himself a double scotch. He sat in his chair looking at the blank notepad with the air of an author in search of a new idea. But on that night, he needed way more than an idea—he needed the complete script, down to the last comma and period.

He had talked Barbara into giving him complete control over cash at Bodega—that was the easy part. The hard part was to do an "Interstate" all over again. He had the confidence that New Horizons would eventually bring in some revenues, but there was a real danger that Bodega would run out of cash before those revenues rolled in. He had to figure out a way to hold the fort till Bodega's profitability improved.

Having learned his lessons at Interstate, George considered the usual ingredients. Revaluation of inventory was out, as Bodega held little or no inventory on hand. Revenue recognition games were out, since Bodega had no revenue to speak of. Window-dressing the accounts receivable was a nonstarter, since nobody really owed anything to Bodega. Mark-to-market tactics, recently championed by some of his friends at Enron, were out, since Bodega held most of its money in plain cash and cash equivalents. The little games he played on deferment of software development expenses got him nowhere.

No matter how George looked it at, it all came back down to basics. To show profits at Bodega, he had to boost revenues or cut costs. But he was done cutting and hiding costs, so the solution had to lie in jacking up revenues. He needed to land a huge new contract, a whopping $50 million boost to Bodega's numbers over the next couple of years.

George began writing down his thoughts. As an inspiration turned into a plot and progressed to a plan, George knew he couldn't pull it off alone. He needed help. Not from someone like Clara who traded favors from time to time but from someone who could work with him on a daily basis. A trustworthy partner with good business smarts and nerves of steel.

He picked up the phone and called, of all places, South Korea.

"*Anyŏnghaseyo*, Mr. Bahng."

"Maestro! Are you about to fly to Seoul on business?"

"No, but I'm calling you on business. Have some time to talk?"

"If it's business," Myeng said, "I have the whole day for you."

"I need someone—well, you really—to buy software technology from Bodega. A $50 million sale."

"Wait a minute, why I should I buy technology at all, let alone from you?"

"Well," George said, "it isn't like I want you to write me a check for fifty million. I'm asking you to sign an agreement for technology transfer, on easy credit, with payments starting in two or maybe three years."

Myeng remained silent at the other end. "Hmm," he said at last. "Things aren't going too well for you, huh?"

"You're a mind reader. Why do you think I called you?"

"Frankly, George, I can't believe *you* came up with this."

George sighed. "I don't *want* to do it, Myeng. But sometimes you gotta do what you gotta do."

"Oh, I didn't mean that way." Myeng laughed. "Come on, you know I'm not a Boy Scout either. My problem is, I can't sell this story to our guys. It took me all of ten seconds to see through it."

"That's because I told you the truth. Wait till you hear the Walt Disney version."

"What?"

"There's a lot to say." George lowered his voice. "And there's something for the two of us as well."

Myeng laughed again. "You haven't changed much."

"So...got a notepad handy?"

"I always do. Let's start."

George began explaining the details. As he talked, he could see in his mind's eye the ever-studious Myeng taking notes at a steady pace like he used to in business school. That was one thing George had always liked about Myeng: the man paid incredible attention to detail.

"So what do you think?" George asked when he was done.

"Let's see," Myeng said, "so far we've got a strategic partnership, investment plans over ten years, hedges against currency fluctuations, marketing rights for South Seas on Bodega software, possible equity participation in the future, and a subsidiary for us in Silicon Valley—"

"So how does it sound now? Is it still a sham that you could see thorough in ten seconds, or is it a worthwhile strategic opportunity for South Seas?"

"Maestro, I've said this before and I'm saying it again: To listen to you is to get educated."

"Thank you. So what do you think?"

"Like always, you seem to have thought through everything. But I need to check with the big guys."

"You aren't going to tell them everything, are you?"

"Come on," Myeng said, "we want them to approve the plan, not understand it!"

"Good," George said. "How much time you need?"

"It'll take a day or two just to get the key players in one room. Then we have to—"

"Can you get back to me same day, same time next week? I just need a high-level approval for now."

"Sure. In fact, I'm shooting for four days."

"Atta boy. You know where to reach me. Call me any time if you need me. Nothing is more important to me these days."

"I know. I'll call you soon, hopefully with good news. When you hang up the phone, I'm going straight to the chairman."

"*Kamsahamnida,* Mr. Bahng."

Four days later, when his cell phone rang at an ungodly hour, George instantly tensed. When Myeng delivered the good news, he tensed even more. They talked till dawn.

George caught hold of Barbara first thing in the morning. "Barb," he said, "please cancel all your meetings for the day."

"Is this about—"

George nodded.

"Should I close the door?"

"No, let's go to my office. I've drawn up a few things over there."

Barbara sat quietly as George went over the plan, often explaining things over and over.

"Well, that's all I've got," he said at last.

"Hmm…so what's next, George?"

George looked at his watch. "We should meet Steve this afternoon. I believe he's got a big decision to make."

"This afternoon? God, this is all moving so fast."

"Much better than not moving at all."

Barbara and George drove up to Santa Cruz to meet Steve at his residence. As they sat on the deck taking in the sweeping views of the Pacific Ocean, Barbara began. "Steve, we've got a problem. And before you ask, yes, we have a plan. We want to run the whole thing by you."

Barbara went on for a few minutes, and just as George had expected, she was soon out of her depth and looked at George. That's when he began.

When he was done, he and Barbara looked expectantly at Steve.

"Well," Steve said, "I like the idea of a strategic partnership with a Korean conglomerate. Obviously, there's a lot of value in going global. As for the details, George, I'm not sure I followed everything you said. I'm not an accountant."

No one spoke another word of business. They sipped some exceedingly nice wine that Steve's personal sommelier had just fetched from his cellar and quietly watched as the sun set in the Pacific.

George called Tom that night. "Start buying up Bodega," he said.

"Will do. Anything else?"

"Be careful and don't get too greedy."

"Trust me," Tom said, "I know how this works."

George sighed as he hung up. He'd had to make that call. Not to pay back Clara for any previous favors but for the huge favor he might have to ask her for a year or two down the road. Just in case.

Pursuit of Happiness

"Something on your mind?" Sam asked.

"Nothing," Kelly said, reaching out for a piece of toast.

"Ah, so there *is* something on your mind."

Kelly laughed. "You *do* know your women. Not bad for a geek." She fell silent, cutting her toast into small pieces with her knife. "Well, I was thinking about…us."

"You know how I feel about you, but why now? You know I have tons of work."

"You *always* have tons of work."

Sam got up and sat next to her. "Kelly, I don't want you to worry. I've got it all figured out. Just let me finish this project and—"

She sighed. "When will you stop burning the candle at both ends? Look at you. When was the last time you had a good night's sleep?"

"You know how important this is to me. I've been working my tail off for years so I could look back at something and say, 'I did that.' Come on, isn't that the reason why you like me in the first place? You want me to take my eyes of the ball now, at a time when everything is falling into place? I mean, without

New Horizons, what am I? Just an average geek doing average work."

"You aren't at all average. If you were average, you'd be leaving work by 5 every day."

"And what's there to show for all that 'not at all average' work? I've delivered nothing so far. *Nothing!*"

"Is that the only thing that matters? Look at the people you know at work. Don't they all like you?"

"Oh, they do—all three of them."

Kelly held his hand. "Sam, don't be so hard on yourself. You know what? Sometimes it's enough to be liked by *one* person you know."

Sam fell silent, wondering what to say. He knew her words shouldn't have come as a surprise, but strangely enough, once the words were out, he was unprepared to respond.

"You have to do what you have to do," Kelly said at last. "I guess I'll wait, but please promise me, Sam, that *I* will be your next project."

"And it won't be too long, I promise. I mean, the deadlines are tight as they are, and now you gave me one more reason to deliver it on time."

"Oh, there you go again. Always work, work, work."

"Ted and Eric tell me you guys are making good progress," Barbara said.

Sam nodded.

"Good. The reason I asked to see you, Sam—is there any way you can speed it up? Maybe get your team to work some extra hours, Saturdays?"

"We're already working Saturdays. About Sundays, I can't promise anything without talking to my team, but speaking for myself, I'll do anything I can."

"Always the workaholic. I appreciate that."

"Thanks, Barb."

Sam got up and started walking back to his office, wondering if there was any room at all to speed up things. He had every reason to finish sooner, but on the other hand, he couldn't recollect the last time when anyone on his team had taken any vacation time. He knew Kris hadn't gone to India in a year despite his parents' asking him to visit, and Vick had officially given up his quest for a girlfriend.

As Sam reached his aisle, he saw Vick intently looking at his wristwatch. When it was precisely noon, Vick blurted, "Yes!" and smiled to himself.

"What's going on?" Sam asked.

Vick got up. "It's time to be happy!"

"What?"

In a matter of seconds, a small crowd gathered around Vick, demanding to know why someone was dropping the H-word at work.

"Yes, it's time," Vick said. "Every week, on Wednesday at 12 noon without fail, we'll have officially covered half of our weekly drudge. We are over the hump, and from this point, it's all peace on Earth and joy in the heavens all the way to the weekend. This is a moment that we should celebrate. Don't you see?"

"If I'm looking dazed right now," Sam said, "it's because you delivered us a blinding flash of the obvious."

"What do you mean?"

"First you tell yourself you're happy. Then you get a kick out of the fact that you *are* happy? What could be more recursive? Do you really think it's cool? I got news for you: You didn't quite create a new cult."

"You got fail," Jennifer said.

"Yes, it is a new cult," Vick said. "And I just created it."

"Must you be so incorrigible?" Sam asked.

"Consider the implications," Vick said. "If you join this new faith and embrace the only ritual it requires—the Weekly Wednesday Watch—you're *guaranteed* to feel good once a week. You'll be happy 50 percent of the week, starting Wednesday at noon, no matter what. Tell me, guys, which faith in the world can match that?"

Sam was as perplexed as the rest of the crowd. People of various faiths, nationalities and cultures blankly looked at the new prophet for several seconds, ostensibly comparing his message with whatever beliefs they might be holding on to.

It didn't take them long to form the Order of Wednesday Happiness and unanimously elect Vick the grandmaster for life.

Globalization

"Agenda item 7," Steve said at the board meeting.

George perked up. Agenda item 7 was all about the South Seas deal. So much was riding on it that George had spoken with Barbara before the meeting and ensured that it would be relegated to the seventh spot on the agenda. He'd even seen to it that Barbara took up a lot of time talking through the first six items, leaving little or no time for item 7.

"On balance I think it's a good idea," Charles, one of the board members, said. "The only odd thing is the payment terms we offered. I mean, we have no payments coming in for *two years.* Isn't it a tad generous?"

"Well," Barbara said, "South Seas can buy up similar technology from any of our competitors, and given the state of the market, they'll probably manage even better terms elsewhere. It's George's personal intervention that even got us this far."

"Two questions, George," Charles said. "First, do you own any stock in South Seas? Second, if you had no friends at South Seas, would you still back this deal? No disrespect, I have to ask as a matter of due diligence."

"Appreciate the straight questions," George said. "First, I never owned any stock in South Seas. Now, your second question is a bit hypothetical, but let me answer it anyway. Even if I didn't know Mr. Bahng, I would back this proposal or a similar deal if it were on the table."

"Good," Charles said. "I believe we can go ahead."

And I'm glad you're merely going through the motions. If you took your job seriously, you'd be asking some pertinent questions.

From what he'd gathered from Myeng, it was a big deal for South Seas as well. It went through the usual buildup: First it was leaked to the press, and it was vehemently denied on a daily basis till the day it was officially confirmed. In the end, the news spread quickly, but they hadn't even had to try—anything that involved South Seas was big news in Korea.

While all the *chaebols* were known to be hungry, South Seas was known to be the hungriest of them all. Kim Chin-Hwa, the maverick entrepreneur who had started the business from his college dorm room, had wanted his company to stand out from day one. To that end, he had given it an English name, a very unusual thing in South Korea. Over the decades, he nurtured it into a competent, ruthless and hungry corporation that almost routinely ventured into opportunities that his competitors deemed too risky. His critics—and there were many—maintained that his company was a chaotic and unpredictable place, much like, well, the South Seas. But those remarks mostly fell on deaf ears, because South Seas always delivered.

"You have no idea how big this is for Chairman Kim," Myeng told George during their usual evening phone call. "He extends a personal invitation to all of you to visit us here and sign the partnership agreement."

"I'd love to," George said, "but not now. As for the conference, let's do something cool, a joint meeting hosted from Silicon Valley and South Korea simultaneously. Let's do it over a satellite link."

"Wow, a live satellite conference—that is so twenty-first century! The Chairman will love that… So, George, what are you planning to say at the conference?"

"I won't say a word. Steve and Barbara will do all the talking."

"Of course," Myeng said, laughing. "You like it that way, don't you?"

"See you soon. On satellite TV, that is."

"The partnership with Bodega marked our first foray into software," Chairman Kim said on satellite TV. "In fact, it's any *chaebol's* big foray into business software. For far too long, the forte of the Korean companies has been manufacturing. Our venture into business software, the kind that our American friends pioneered for decades, is a significant step forward. It is practically the last frontier in our nation's struggle to expand our competitive advantage. A big day for South Seas and for Korea as a whole."

As the hacks watched the large video monitor and made notes, he furnished more details. South Seas Corporation was opening offices in Santa Clara, right in the heart of Silicon Valley. Marco Polo Inc. would soon be incorporated as a wholly owned subsidiary of South Seas—the gateway for its business in North America.

"Even in the digital age," Chairman Kim said, "it is important to meet the customer and shake his hand. And on that note, I give it back to our partners at Bodega."

The questions from the press started.

"Can you elaborate on your relationship with the South Seas Corporation?"

"We have a shared vision," Barbara said, "and South Seas is backing that vision by investing heavily in our technology. It is a strategic partnership."

"Will they be marketing your software in Asia-Pac?"

"I can't rule that out," Barbara said with a smile.

"Question to the South Seas Corporation: What would you say to your critics who maintain you take too much risk— more risk than you can prudently handle?"

George smiled to himself. Nothing like a planted question at a press conference. Myeng had begged him to make sure it came up.

"Almost anyone can sail the trade winds," Myeng took that question. "But as you know, the South Seas are different. It takes courage and skill to sail those uncertain waters. But my friends, that's what we are." He paused for effect, leaned over a bit and said slowly and emphatically, "Risk is in our blood."

George couldn't help but smile. *You practice well, my friend.*

George called Myeng later that night.

"That was a good show," George said.

"With you in charge, how could it be anything else?"

"Thanks. So what are you now, a high flier at South Seas?"

"I've been a high flier since the day I joined," Myeng said, "and now I'm a front-runner."

"Front-runner?"

"Yes." Myeng lowered his voice. "Chairman Kim is not going to be the boss forever, you know. He's getting into politics. You notice how speaks when he's on the television—you know, always making that 'big day for Korea' speech? He's building up that image."

"So you're in line for the job?"

"Well, it's a long way to go. But I'll remember this when I get there."

"Glad to hear it." George hung up and launched the browser on his computer. He read everything the press had said on the South Seas deal. One article said:

> It's quite a coup for Bodega. There is so much value locked up in the technology it has in its arsenal, and it is silly to sit on all that intellectual property and not make money on it. In fact, the idea is hardly new. Dolby made a ton of money not by selling an end product but by licensing technology to others. It's to the great credit of Barbara Collins and her management team that they exploit the untapped potential and open up these new revenue streams.

Bodega stock began soaring and continued to do so every day. As always happened with soaring stocks, half a dozen analysts upgraded it to "buy" or "outperform," causing it to soar even more. There was no end to the good news.

"The wheels are in motion," George said as he walked into Barbara's office with the newspaper in his hand.

"Nice to see you smile at last," Barbara said. "God, you had that frown for way too long."

"Couldn't help it, you know."

"Oh, George, you always look out for us. I appreciate it very much."

"Glad to hear it."

"So what's next?"

"Next stop: third-quarter results."

THE SLAVE CLUB

"HEY SAM, WHY DO WE USE the word *deadline* to denote something that keeps moving all the time?"

Tired and sleep deprived, they were leaving after yet another status meeting where they had revised the dates for delivering the New Horizons project one more time. The middle managers had had the usual good reason or two to offer and, as was more often the case, a plethora of plausible excuses to explain away the delays: inter-team dependencies, third-party deficiencies, scope changes, resource issues, unexpected bugs, changed industry standards, the works. So many excuses were offered so frequently that people joked that the management would soon blame it all on global warming.

Everyone worked hard and some worked harder. Staying late was so commonplace that anyone who left before 6 p.m. had to get a prior approval from the boss.

A sense of bonhomie developed among the employees who regularly saw one another working the late hours or through the weekends. These chronic workaholics even formed an informal club: the Slave Club.

Sam and his team soon became card-carrying members of the Slave Club. They ate practically all their meals together. When they chose "slack off a bit" and leave before 8 p.m., they were still together, downing beers at Duncan's.

If any member of the Slave Club chose to leave early on a given day, he was heckled as "slacker of the day." That practice soon developed into a contest—Slacker of the Week—to identify and publicly hang the poor soul who had left a little too early a little too often or hadn't shown up to work on a Saturday, thus denigrating the Slave Club's code of honor.

The competition went up a notch when Vick started entering other people—people who weren't members of Slave Club—into the contest without their knowledge, let alone their consent. For a few weeks, volunteers from the Slave Club spied on the potential slackers to note when they entered and left the building. They compared notes in a secret late-hour meeting on Friday to determine the Slacker of the Week. Then they started placing bets all through the week on the likely winners. The weekly winner was, of course, never let in on his or her dubious distinction, but the Slave Club had its share of perverse fun tracking other people's work hours without their knowledge.

One week, just for kicks, Sam entered Ted's name into the contest, and he won hands down. Per contest rules, any given week's winner automatically qualified as a contestant the following week, and lo and behold, Ted won the following week as well. And on it went.

When Ted was declared Slacker of the Week too many times in a row, everyone in the Slave Club decided that the rules of the contest had to be changed to keep it interesting. At the usual Slave Club secret meeting on Friday evening, there was considerable deliberation about exactly what kind of change was needed.

There was much merriment and general agreement when Vick proposed that, effective immediately, professional slackers be excluded from the contest.

Then they all went back to work.

In between, Sam and friends invented more games. Vick started to deliberately slip a bug or two into the code to see how fast Kris would catch it. Kris was so good at it that the game soon became boring, so they reversed their roles.

One day Jennifer started speaking in pseudo-code, with generous doses of *while, select, if, else, then* and *end*.

"Jen, this is getting to be too much," Vick said. "If you keep talking like that, I won't work with you."

"Else what?" she asked.

One week they all spoke with a Texan accent, though none of them had ever lived in the South. It all went fine till Friday afternoon when Vick suddenly dropped the accent.

"How come y'all don't speak with an accent?" Kris asked him.

"Are you ready for this?" Vick said, sitting up straight and carefully enunciating every syllable. "I have chosen to talk like a TV newsreader all the time. But here's the real question: Is this going to be sustainable? And how does this affect our freedom and our way of life? Don't go away, that's after the break."

"Oh, you want to talk like a newsreader?" Kris said. "How many missing white women do you know?"

"Dude," Vick said, "I don't know what the Immigration Service thinks of you, but in my book, you just qualified for your green card."

***

It was Saturday. Despite the seventy-plus hours they had already clocked that week, Sam and friends were at work. Through the day, amid blaring music of all genres and pizzas of all toppings, they worked on the usual tasks: spec, code, test, retest, debug, document and so on. In the evening, having decided to slack off, the gang of four headed to Duncan's. They sat on the patio, taking in the cool breeze, the cold beer and the hot wings.

"Man, we have been working way too hard," Sam said.

"Wow, that's so perceptive of you," Vick said. "Really, what was your first clue?"

"Dude, get off my back for ten minutes while I enjoy my beer, all right?"

Vick backed off and turned toward Kris. "What about you, man? Do you think it's worthwhile, coming here all the way from India and working these crazy hours?"

"Man, I never worked this hard in my whole life," Kris said. "But on the other hand, nobody forced me to come here, and basically I like what I'm doing. So, in the end—"

"In the end, is your glass half-full or half-empty?" Sam asked, with a mock reference to the drink Kris was holding.

"In America, the glass is neither full nor empty," Kris said. "It is buy one, get one free."

SEC, Lies and Financial Results

"WE'VE HAD MANY FALSE DAWNS in the Valley," Barbara said, "but it's finally daybreak at Bodega. In these times, with so much blood on the streets, we report Bodega's best quarter ever."

She continued for many minutes in that vein during the post-earnings conference call, giddy about the blowout quarter Bodega had just reported.

"This good news is made possible by the hard-working men and women of Bodega," she said. "Seven years ago, we were just a few individuals with a dream. Now it is all a reality. We are better poised than ever to serve the ever-changing needs of the marketplace… We are, of course, a new-economy company, but a few old-fashioned things never change, such as the obligation to make a profit for our investors. On that note, I hand it over to my colleague and CFO, George Stevenson."

George spoke softly and at a steady pace befitting the "numbers guy" and presented the key numbers: the revenues, expenses, deferred items, one-time charges and, yes, the good ol' profit.

Then it was back to Barbara. She talked about aggressive growth and possible new revenue streams. "Thanks to our new strategic partners, we should have no problem in meeting the new earnings guidance that we just shared."

One of analysts asked the question, exactly as George had planted it: "You've mentioned aggressive growth as your go-forward strategy. Are you going to raise fresh capital?"

"Not necessarily. Generally speaking, we don't want to dilute our equity base. But remember, Lou, we can't always neglect growth at the expense of profitability. So, if need be, we may tap into the market for fresh capital. But we really have no plans at the moment."

"A giddy Barbara Collins reports a blowout quarter," the online news said right after the earnings call. George couldn't help but smile. The conference call couldn't have gone any better. They'd reported profits, and they'd said the right things about the need to raise fresh capital without looking desperate. As they said on the street, if you really want the money, first make it clear to everyone that you don't need the money.

George learned from Myeng that the South Seas Corporation had announced its financial results in South Korea. There was hardly any mention of its American operations in its books. On a multibillion-dollar financial statement, George figured, there was no way a $50 million new investment in business software would figure prominently. But Myeng assured him that when it came to the vision and mission part, Marco Polo was mentioned prominently. Chairman Kim had even made the usual "we've come a long way" speech.

"We've come a long way?" George said. "Did he really say that?"

"His political prospects are looking better and better,"

Myeng said. "All the more reason to talk like that whenever he's in the public eye. But George, he's right in a way."

"Really?"

Myeng filled him in on the details. The way the chairman saw it, it was all about hardware versus software. Thanks to decades of backbreaking work, the Koreans had become pretty good at hardware, but in the end, it meant that a worker still had to put a widget together, ship it and do it all over again with the next widget. The new-economy American worker did it differently. Once a piece of code was written and tested, the software license was sold over and over again, bringing in an endless stream of revenue.

"So, we make it once and sell it once," Myeng said. "You Americans make it once and sell it a million times. Sounds simple, but in the end that's the only business model where America can still compete with the rest of the world. Chairman Kim wants Korea to get there soon."

"Your chairman is a shrewd man. Be careful about what you tell him."

While Barbara was basking in the limelight of favorable press coverage, George was sweating over a little detail that nobody had bothered to notice on the earnings call.

His high-wire act had begun two weeks earlier, when Bodega announced the financial results and declared a "profit." All that profit had come from the technology sale to Korea. It was a sale, but only on paper, with no cash coming in. George shared the usual key figures at the earnings call, but he carefully left out the details on cash flow, with the promise of making it available later. While that omission was not a scandal in itself, nor was it an outright crime, it was definitely a case of being economical with the truth.

He had gone through that conference call with his heart pounding, hoping no one would ask about the cash flow, because Bodega was bleeding cash as ever, even in a "blowout" quarter. As if by magic, nobody asked the question. But then, it was *his* magic.

"When you open the conference," he had told Barbara the day before the earnings call, "take charge. You've got tons of good news to share. Bowl them over with the results. Wow them when you give the guidance. Make a few self-deprecating jokes so you come across as confident and reassuring."

"Relax," Barbara said. "I can handle good news."

When Barbara went all giddy with the results and guidance, every analyst on the call clamored for her attention and no one bothered to ask anything of the bean counter. As happened in any magic show, when the magician said, "Look here, look here," the audience looked only there and nowhere else.

It worked—at least for the moment. George knew he had to carry the show for a few quarters and hope no one asked the question he feared most. And once New Horizons started to make some real money, he could window-dress the results and absorb it back into the earlier "profits" just like he had at Interstate.

It could work like magic as long as nobody asked any questions, or it could all come down in an instant. As he knew only too well, the first cracks in Enron's financial fortress had appeared when people started asking the right questions, and the good life ended for many of his buddies over there in a matter of days.

"You know, Myeng, sometimes I'm surprised how well this is working out," George told him over the phone. "No trouble at all. Not one thing went wrong."

"I guess this is how all the homework pays off."

"It's too soon, my friend, too soon to say that. We have to give it a year at least. Even then it will be far from over."

"George, in case someone asks you, 'Hey, you sold software to Korea—where's the money from the proceeds?' what are you going to say?"

"Oh, that. I have an internal memo that says we gave you generous terms of credit on account of you being a significant strategic partner. It even has the board approval."

"Ah, I *knew* you would do something on those lines. But I must confess I get scared at times, when I think of Wall Street. Seriously, George, did you expect them to just lap it up?"

"You want to know what happened to these analysts? They've all become so obsessed with reading between the lines that they've stopped reading the lines."

"What can I say? I feel educated."

George hung up and ran his numbers for the umpteenth time. After all the mind-numbing analysis involving front companies, subsidiaries of overseas corporations, cash-flow projections for the next eight quarters and circuitous business transactions for the foreseeable future, he wrote down the new mantra for Bodega, to be rigorously followed henceforth till a decent level of profitability was attained:

Boost revenues and cut costs.

The next morning, George got hold of Barbara.

"Hi, George!" she said, stretching and reclining in her office chair. "God, at last a quiet day at the office. God, can't remember when I last had one of those… So what's up?"

"Two things," George said. "And we gotta move fast."

"Oh, for God's sake, we just had a blowout quarter. And we *will* raise the extra money you asked for. Give it a rest and chill out a little, all right?"

I asked you to tell everyone we had a blowout quarter. I didn't say we should believe in it ourselves. "Barb, it isn't over till it's over."

She looked at him for a moment and then sat straight in her chair. "Guess you're right. All right then, what do we do?"

"We've got to have a salable product ASAP. We've got to deploy New Horizons, even if it isn't 100 percent ready."

"Well, Sam and his team are going full steam anyway. Oh, by the way, I gather from Ted that they're running into some issues with our outside partners, mainly the cell phone service providers, I gather."

"You don't want to hear any of that. We've got to ship something soon. If there are technical glitches, don't spend too much time solving them. Just find a work-around we can all live with. Cut back the features, lose a few bells and whistles, do whatever it takes. We need *revenue,* Barb. I can't hold the fort forever."

"Okay then, I'll talk to them. Anything else?"

"We have to cut a few costs."

"What? Haven't you done that many times already?"

Cutting costs is a bit like cleaning the kitchen, Barb. You have to keep doing it.

George didn't reply. He went back to his office and resumed his work. After years of relentless cuts, the only thing left was to slay whole departments: The market research, sales and business analysis teams could be rolled into one department, making many jobs redundant. Development and quality assurance could also be merged into one. All that could cut the head count by a third.

Having engineered a plan for reducing the head count by the busload, he paused to think about what to call it. He was hell-bent on *not* calling it a headcount reduction or a reorg or anything else that sounded remotely negative. He wanted to give it a name that wouldn't be deemed newsworthy even if someone leaked it to the press.

After some deliberation, he settled on "the Quality Improvement Plan." Then he put the wheels in motion.

Memo to Geeks: You Don't Matter

Sam couldn't believe what he'd just heard. Reduce the head count? Everyone was working crazy hours already—who was he going to eliminate?

He had slept for all of four hours the night before, and like always he had come in early so he could do some prep work before his team arrived. The last thing he needed was an impromptu meeting with Barbara and Ted on downsizing his team.

"But Barb," Sam said, "there's no way I can reduce the head count. Everyone on my team has a specific role to fill. We lose one person and the whole project will be crippled for months."

"But this is a company-wide initiative," Ted said. "We're expecting *every* project to comply, no exceptions."

Oh, I see. Was I supposed to keep a couple of losers on my team to be disposed of at short notice and wait for you to start a "company-wide initiative" so I could comply?

"Sam?"

"I obviously can't speak for the other projects," Sam said, struggling to keep an even tone. "But on New Horizons, I just can't reduce the head count."

"Oh, that's what they all say. But this is a company-wide initiative. All teams must comply, no exceptions."

This isn't helping. Sam turned toward Barbara. "Remember, Barb? You said I could pick my team. How can I lose control of my team in the middle of the project?"

Barbara shifted uncomfortably in her chair and turned toward Ted.

"She might have said so," Ted said before Barbara could speak, "but you know things can change on a daily basis. Come on, you gotta fine-tune the plans as you go, you gotta be *adaptive.* It's the new economy!"

Oh great, now you get to lecture me on the new economy.

"Don't just keep looking at me, all right?" Ted said. "Give me a reason why you can't cut the head count."

"As you say," Sam said, "things can change on a daily basis in the new economy. Which is exactly why we need to have qualified people on the team. Otherwise we won't be able to cope with any changes in the marketplace."

"Sam," Barbara said, "I think you've made a valid observation. But still, there's always room for improvement, right?"

"Yes, continuous improvement," Ted said. "Look at Eric. He's cutting his team on the business side. Why can't you do that on the technical side?"

Sam remained silent for a moment while he absorbed that piece of information. *So they asked Eric to cut his team and he didn't even mention it to me?*

"Yeah, we asked Eric and he's delivering," Ted continued. "He didn't make excuses on how 'the whole thing would collapse.' And this project is *his* idea to begin with."

"Ted, please," Barbara said.

"Barb," Sam said, "I don't know why or how Eric can cut his team. Speaking for the technical side, I just can't cut my team."

"That's it?" Ted asked.

Sam took a deep breath and looked at Ted. "Yes. I promised to deliver the solution on time, and I can't do that if you cut my team."

Ted didn't reply. He stared at Sam, looking angrier than ever and as confused as ever.

"Okay, Sam," Barbara said at last, "I think we're okay for now. Please put all this behind and go back to your team. Oh, by the way, keep this to yourself, okay? Not a word to anyone."

"Sure."

As he walked downstairs, Sam thought about what he'd heard. *What's behind this move for headcount reduction? And what's going on with Eric? How can he possibly cut his team?*

"Honest!" Eric said. "It's not like I chose to keep it from you. They piled on me big time, man, so I *had to* agree. That's really all that happened. You know I work sixteen hours a day, so I suppose you don't blame me for not finding the time to share everything with you."

"Don't get me wrong, I believe you," Sam said. "I learned it from Barb, and I was caught off-guard, that's all."

"Ah."

"So you're cutting your team? I mean, you guys are over-worked as is."

"I don't *want* to, but on balance it's best to give them what they want, even if you disagree personally. We aren't here to pick fights, man; we're here to get things done."

"I can't cut my team," Sam said. "That's the truth and that's exactly what I told them."

Eric shook his head. "You be careful, all right?"

***

"They're cutting costs *everywhere*," Sam said. "No, no, not *our* team, like I said. But Ted and Barbara are going after everyone. It just doesn't make sense."

"When did cutting costs stop making sense?" Vick asked.

"No, that's not what I mean. Look, Bodega has gone through a turnaround—we *are* making a profit—yet there are layoffs everywhere. One would think we're bleeding money. It just doesn't add up."

"So you have a conspiracy theory to explain all this? Do yourself a favor and stop watching the History Channel."

"Guys, guys," Jennifer said, "it doesn't take a conspiracy theory to explain what's going on. You see, it goes back to the basics: supply and demand."

"What do you mean?" Sam asked.

"Just look around the Valley, outside our office. There's blood on the streets. Businesses are folding and people are getting laid off. Face it—we're no longer the royalty of Silicon Valley. So what do they do with more geeks out on the streets than there are job openings?"

"I see where you're going with this," Vick said. "Of course, they'll want to squeeze the hell out of us now."

"Correction," Jennifer said. "The big guys *always* wanted to squeeze the hell out of us, but they couldn't do it till now. And now they can—so they will."

"So what's next?" Vick asked.

"What's next," Jennifer said, "is that we've got to hunker down and watch out. Who knows? We could be next."

"No way," Sam said. "I told you, our project is top priority."

"But you know how it is," Vick said. "One day they tell us we're top priority and the next day they throw us out like garbage."

"Not this time," Sam said. "I know for sure New Horizons

won't be killed. You know why? We're making money just by selling the Pandora *technology* to South Seas. Can you imagine what we could do with all that technology packaged into a *finished product*?"

"What if they keep the project but get rid of us?" Vick said.

"Who'll do our job then?" Sam asked. "They can play their politics all day, but the simple truth is, no one else around here can do our job."

A day later, Ted sent out a company-wide e-mail about the impending reorganization. In part, it said:

> As we continue to sail through the ever-changing business environment, it is imperative for us to pay particular attention to the quality of our processes and, by extension, the quality our products. The Quality Improvement Plan will aim to facilitate fewer hand-overs between teams, less communication meltdowns and, most important, boost our worker productivity… At all levels in this company, the contribution to Quality Improvement will be considered a Key Performance Indicator for this year.

"Oh, *Ted* is talking quality," Jennifer said. "Ted! When was the last time he cared about quality or anything else, for that matter?"

"Actually, we never had big quality problems," Kris said. "Minor glitches, of course, but nothing serious."

"Does anyone know what they're talking about?" Sam asked.

"Yes," Vick said, "I can tell you exactly what this is all about."

"Oh yeah?"

"That's an e-mail from the top management."

"So?"

"So it's all about money. No matter what they're talking about, they're talking about money, particularly when they pretend it's not about the money."

"It's not about the money," Ted opened the meeting. "I don't know where this misconception came from. As you all know, all our projects are adequately funded. But on the other hand, we have to focus on quality and continuous improvement…"

The meeting ended earlier than scheduled, leaving Sam wondering what really was going on at Bodega. Quality had never been a problem. Nobody ever said a word about quality, even in private, but why was Ted talking about it in public? When exactly had it become a problem?

Long after everyone left the meeting room, Sam sat there alone, trying to collect his thoughts. *When it finally looks like I'm getting where I wanted to be, I can't figure out what's going on a mere fifty feet from my desk.*

Don't Eat the Menu

"Good morning, everyone. Let's get started," Ted began the meeting. "Turns out that New Horizons is running into a few problems with our industry partners."

Sam looked at Ted and Eric in disbelief, but neither of them made eye contact with him. *I thought things had been moving well. What have you been hiding from me?*

"Before we dig deeper," Ted continued, "let me remind you of the rules of the game. Please discuss the issues, not the people. We are here to solve problems, not to fix the blame."

Then you must've screwed up. Of course you start off by saying it's not a blame game.

"We've been getting quite some pushback from the phone companies," Ted said. "The cell phone establishment wants to keep more control on what can be run from a phone. I don't think they've caught on to the idea of third-party developers yet. So we have two choices: Keep pushing the phone companies or bypass them by taking the cell phone out of the equation."

"Yikes!"

"These things happen, unfortunately," Ted continued. "There'll always be setbacks. We just have to plan for contingencies, which is exactly what we did."

"So what's the fallback?" Sam asked, trying hard to keep an even tone. *You gave me no notice. How could you drop me into this?*

"I was coming to that," Ted said. "Instead of using the cell phone, the users will simply launch their web browser on their laptops and order groceries over the web. While it's not as 'cool' as ordering things from a cell phone, it still provides great value and convenience to the customer."

"What about the setbacks to development time?" someone asked.

"We actually *save* time, that's the whole point. We're reducing the scope so we can deploy the solution without waiting on third parties."

"So we ship it sooner?"

"Yes," Ted said, beaming at everyone. "And the best part is, unlike the cell phone stuff, nobody really owns the Internet. As long as we adhere to the Internet protocols, we can do what we like. Good news overall."

Sam looked at him in disbelief. *This is good news? You reduced a cool idea to a run-of-the-mill idea in ten minutes and this is somehow good news?* He looked at Ted and Eric. Eric averted his eyes, a bit shamefaced.

"Sam," Ted said, "we'll come to you in a moment. But from a strategic perspective, we still deliver a core benefit to the consumer. Compared to sweating it out at the grocery store, it's still a good idea. Eric, you have anything to add?"

"Things are always unpredictable like Ted explained," Eric said, still trying to avoid any eye contact with Sam. "We have to adapt. You know, it's like being a restaurant chef. The customer walks in and orders fajitas. You as a chef have to improvise sometimes, depending on what's fresh and what's available: green peppers instead of red peppers, rice pilaf instead of Mexican rice and so on. But as long the meal is delivered on time, who cares about these little deviations from the plan? Let's face it—in the end, the customer wants a meal. He doesn't eat the menu—"

"Excuse me," Sam said, his voice louder than usual and in a tone that clearly surprised many. "Two questions. One: Why didn't you see it coming? Two: Why wasn't I kept in the loop?"

"Good questions," Ted said, nodding sagely.

"Then please answer them!" Sam said. "You can't call a meeting out of the blue and basically rewrite everything in a matter of minutes!"

Barbara spoke up before Sam could go further. "Sam, I know you have some concerns, but I ask you to take this topic offline with me. Let's focus on what concerns the whole team, okay?"

"But this *does* concern the whole team."

"Sam, *please.*"

Oh great, what's next? I'm not a "team player" anymore? Sam looked at Ted and Eric, wondering what to say next, but they were both looking at Barbara, all too grateful for her "managing" the situation.

"Sam," Barbara continued, "I know you're upset, and let's meet up right after this meeting. Now, Ted and Eric, I can't say I like what I heard today, but overall I'm happy that you're managing this contingency very well. I appreciate that. But in the end, I must insist on delivering the product ASAP. As always, thank you for all the hard work."

***

"Sam," Barbara said, "Ted is leading the project overall, and Eric is on the business side—it's their call to make changes to scope as they deem fit."

"Not when it fundamentally changes the project. What they did is hasty and inappropriate."

"But they aren't adding anything to your work. If anything, they're taking away a lot of work, making your life a little easier. You've been working way too hard as it is… Come on, don't get too hung up on what *you* want this to be. Let's face it—it's Eric's idea to begin with. Let him handle the scope."

Sam sighed. *Maybe I should've told you it was my idea, too. Now it's too late.*

"Don't take it too hard," Barbara said. "Who knows? Maybe the phone companies will come around and then we could go back and add the phone back into the project."

Sam perked up a bit. If only for a moment, he wanted to believe his vision would come true one day. But he realized Barbara was trying to "manage" this situation, too. He remained silent.

"See?" Barbara was saying, "I knew you'd come around and be positive as always, which is why I wanted you to be the development manager in the first place… Sam, you know what's most important for Bodega at the moment? To *deploy* the solution in the real world. Once that happens, we get credibility in the market and everyone will see things our way. Then, who knows? We could add back the pieces we removed today."

Sam thought about it. It made sense, except that he was no longer sure he could believe everything Barbara said. Or even Eric. He got up from his chair.

"Hope there are no hard feelings," Barbara said. "I really like having you around."

Helpdesk

Happy hour at Duncan's was winding down a bit, but Kris was showing no signs of slowing down. Sam had stopped after four drinks and Vick and Jen had already left, but Kris reached out for his sixth beer as if it was his first in a month.

"Here's to life," Kris said, raising his glass.

"Thanks for trying to cheer me up," Sam said.

"I wasn't trying to cheer you up. My point is that you should feel good anyway."

"I should feel good? After what happened today? How many beers have you had exactly?"

"Enough beers to look at things rationally. Seriously, Sam, you should sometimes step back a bit and look at things from a distance."

"What's your point?"

Kris took a big gulp of his beer. "You know why I came to America?"

"Dude, you completely lost me."

"It will be clear in a minute, but first answer this: When was the last time America did something cool? I mean really, really cool? That happened in the *sixties*, man, when you put a man on the moon. After that, what did you do? You lost a military war to Vietnam, suffered through an oil shock and then lost an economic war to Japan. That's really all you guys did for a *whole freaking generation.* And then—fast-forward to the nineties and you're back in charge. You guys are cool again, all thanks to the Internet…which is why *I* came to work here."

"I see, but—"

"What is America without the new economy and all these new ideas? Yet another nation of aging people. Just a fatter, dumber version of Japan."

"Oh, I see," Sam said. "So I should 'distance myself from what happened today' and forget what happened? I don't think so."

"I'm not asking you to forget it," Kris said. "I'm asking you not to take it so hard. Seriously, Sam, what we do here is important. Look at you—people will be able to stock up their homes *like never before,* thanks to your design… Just a few months from now, you'll be able to look back at something and say, 'I did that.'"

"You touched a soft spot there."

"Change the world, I know. I know how you feel about today's setback. So what? You can go shout at Ted and Eric all you want, but what will that achieve?"

Sam didn't reply. He kept thinking about what Eric had said to him that afternoon. "They piled on me big time, man," he'd said. "Barb and Ted told me to change the design and ship something in two months or else. Ted asked me where we can cut the scope and I ended up saying we could take the phone out of picture. And then we all walked into the meeting and you know the rest. Sam, I had no time at all to tell you what was going on. Honest, man, they really piled on."

133

Sam looked at Kris.

"You have to give in sometimes," Kris said. "Changing the world is a journey, not a goal."

Changing the world is a journey, not a goal. If I heard that two years ago, I would've dismissed it as some pretentious bull, fit for a motivational poster in the cafeteria. But it makes sense now. Only a little, but it makes sense.

"Look at me," Kris said. "Can you even imagine what all *I* had to give up to pursue my dreams?"

"I know." Sam sighed. "Sometimes I wonder if *I* could ever leave behind everything and move to the other end of the world."

"But you shouldn't have to. Take it from a guy who took *two* transcontinental flights just to get here. You're already in the right place at the right time. You're still chasing your dreams. You're still changing the world. And Bodega is still your helpdesk."

"Thanks, man, I appreciate it."

"Atta boy," Kris said in his best American accent.

Sam laughed. "Your English has always been good, but your accent is a whole different story."

"One out of two isn't bad. On that happy note, let me get you a beer."

"No." Sam rose from his chair. "I think I'll get back to work."

Fifteen Weeks
of Fame

Sam and friends walked into the cafeteria. Many of the Bodega employees were already there, along with a few members of the press. In a while, Barbara took the stage amid much cheering.

"There is lots of good news to share," she said. "First and foremost, our much-promised project New Horizons is now ready for commercial deployment. Starting next month, consumers in Santa Clara and Cupertino can start ordering groceries over the Internet."

Sam watched as many people he had known for years clapped and cheered. Many pointed at him as if to say, "You're the man."

"All this is just the beginning," Barbara said. "With selling groceries, we now have a technology demonstrator that can be leveraged to sell a variety of things. Perhaps movie tickets. Maybe even a laundry pickup and delivery service—I, for one, can't wait for that service to begin…"

Soon it was time for questions, which came mostly from the press.

"Don't we already have some players in the markets you mentioned?" someone asked. "Movie tickets, for example?"

"Yes," Barbara said, "but we have international exposure, thanks to our strategic partners at South Seas. Can you imagine the kind of reach we'll have in the Far East? In fact, consumers over there adapt to new technology way better than us! We're sitting on a gold mine here."

"Are you going to license your technology to others?"

"We're doing that already, with South Seas. Perhaps we'll expand that in the near future. And we're looking at many other options around leveraging New Horizons. Beyond that…well, I'm not saying anything."

Steve was there, too, and he was in his element, shaking hands with everyone in sight and throwing in an occasional backslap for the chosen few.

When the meeting ended, Sam got up to leave, but a familiar voice stopped him.

"Sam, don't slip away without saying hello."

Sam turned to see Steve beaming at him. They shook hands.

"Good job," Steve said. "Aren't you happy how things turned out?"

"Of course. I've been waiting for this day for a long time."

"Change the world, I know. You've finally done it."

Yes, but I meant taking the weekend off and taking Kelly to Lake Tahoe.

Soon the marketing blitz began. Every day, there was a story or two in the press or an enticing ad on television or an online opinion maker posting something favorably. The *Cupertino Chronicle* wrote:

> All the years of hard work by the finest minds in Silicon Valley are not lost. There is something to show

for it. After all the disheartening stories about the dotcom bust, there is revival. From booking airline tickets we've progressed to trading air miles online; from reading movie reviews online we've moved on to booking tickets. Buying groceries is a natural step in the progression. In a market full of pessimism and false dawns, Bodega InfoTech is a refreshing ray of hope.

Barbara was hailed as the visionary behind the success. There were stories about her in the press, her name was regularly listed among the nation's "power women" and she even delivered the keynote speech at a glitzy conference or two.

Shareholders rejoiced at the newly resurgent stock and started to post favorable comments on the online investing forums. People who had sold off their Bodega stock in previous years cursed themselves and bought into the stock afresh. It rose day after day, much to the heart-pounding of the shareholders and much to the heartburn of anyone who had missed out on the most happening stock of the year.

"Man, I am so happy," Sam said, raising his third beer at Duncan's.

"I've yet to meet a man who isn't happy to drink beer," Vick said.

"Come on, you know what I mean."

"Of course. What's not to like? For three years—four years, I think—we didn't have much of a life. At last there's something to show for it."

"Very true," Sam said. "How nice it is to meet your goals while you're still in your twenties."

"Let's drink to that," Vick said. After a few seconds, he added, "Hey, it's not over yet."

"I know."

"I'm starting first thing tomorrow morning on the bugs. You know, Sam, I still think we shipped the whole thing a bit too early. And I'm not alone. Kris was complaining all day."

"I'm with you. In fact, I went up to Barbara and told her as much, not once but many times. But no matter how many times I brought it up, she kept saying, 'Yeah, there are always some bugs in any software, but you can always fix them later.' And you know what? I don't think it was *her* idea to ship the product this fast."

"Hmm. Then whose idea was it?"

"Barbara won't name any names, but she mentioned finance," Sam said.

"George?"

"If I were to guess, I'd say it's George. But what's the point? The finance guys don't talk to us anyway. To cut a long story short, they told Ted and Eric to ship the product and then fix the bugs or else."

"I never liked George," Vick said.

"I don't either. And the funny part is, I don't know *why*. I just can't put my finger on it."

"We rarely get to see him and never get to talk to him. And yet *he* and his buddies upstairs are calling the shots on everything. That's reason enough. To tell you the truth, I have a feeling this isn't going to end well."

"Dude."

"Okay, I said my piece. Let me go get some more beer."

We Wrote the Code,
Not the Law

It all started as a trickle, with a few complaining voices from consumers and Ted and Eric explaining them away at the deployment review meeting as "the usual post go-live issues."

"I've seen this over and over," Eric said. "The American consumer has been conditioned to complain no matter what. Give Joe Consumer a complimentary ride into outer space and he'll still complain. He'll whine about how hard it is to get some sleep out there and how weird it is to use the bathroom in zero gravity."

Right on cue, Ted nodded sagely, looking around the room.

"Still, we've got to fix the glitches," Sam said. "Remember, these are the *known* problems. What about the unknown? We've got to slow down a bit."

"What are you suggesting?"

"Why do you want to roll out the solution to Palo Alto when we have people in Santa Clara complaining about it?" Sam said. "Let's hold back a bit, let the whole system stabilize and then we can resume the rollout."

"No," Eric said. "You don't forgo new business just because there are a few dissenting voices here and there. I just told you about the consumer mentality. Going back to our Joe Consumer, I'm sure he'll find it all a distasteful experience because, up there in outer space when you brush your teeth, you don't spit, but... you have to swallow it all."

Ted made a face. "I didn't know that."

The meeting ended with that little insight into space shuttle hygiene.

But the complaints kept coming—now from Palo Alto as well.

A few customers, mostly small business owners, received the goods at their *office addresses* when they wanted the delivery to be at their *home addresses*. It was eventually traced to a bug; the program didn't always distinguish the correct delivery address from the billing address. It was a stupid glitch—Sam and Vick fixed it in no time—but from a customer's viewpoint, the damage had been done.

The grocery stores, for their part, made an occasional minor mistake such as substituting Fiji apples for Honey Crisp apples. Topping it off were a few human errors, such as picking up the wrong product from the bins—they mixed up, quite literally, apples and oranges. And it was all quickly attributed to the "new system."

Even when things went right, they weren't entirely good. A few stores, in a fit of better inventory management through "better use of technology," started to ship out milk that was just about to expire. Word spread online like wildfire, and with every chat board highlighting the "pitfalls of buying things over the Internet," customers started restricting their online purchases to soap, shampoo, mineral water and other nonperishables. Then they stopped buying online altogether, as they were shopping in stores anyway for the perishables. Soon the online deliveries slowed to a trickle. The delivery fleet, in more ways than one, wasn't getting anywhere.

Then came the legal issues.

One day as the delivery van rolled onto a sleepy boulevard to deliver a crate of beer, a group of excited teenagers answered the door. When the delivery guy asked for proof of age, they showed a fake ID and tipped him well. All in all, it was the digital equivalent of underage guys showing up at a bar with fake IDs, but when the media learned of the story, they turned it into the story of a huge pitfall of the *Internet*.

"Bodega wrote the code," Sam said at the review meeting. "And the code does remind the user to check for ID when delivering beer. It's even printed on the route manifest, for God's sake! I tested it myself and I know it works. How can *we* be responsible if they don't follow the procedure?"

"What do you suggest?" Barbara asked.

"We should go talk to the DA's office, and to the press. Let's make our position clear."

"No," Eric said. "We're talking legal issues here. We've got to be careful. Never, ever go to the DA's office on your own and make a statement. No matter what we say, they'll find something in it to indict us."

"Eric has a point there," Barbara said. "The less we say to the DA's office, the less they have on us."

"But what do we have to fear?" Sam said. "It's the others who broke the law. Why is it our fault?"

"I'm not disputing what you say," Eric said. "The problem is, there are no guarantees that the DA's office will see it the same way you do. Our best hope is that the stores are let off with a citation or a penalty and the kids are given a bit of counseling, and hopefully everyone puts this behind and moves on."

"So we do *nothing?*" Sam asked.

"Man, we wrote the code. We aren't responsible for what happened. You said so yourself. Let's leave it there and see what happens."

But the district attorney, apparently, saw things differently. He named pretty much everyone in the beer-to-teenagers transaction chain, perhaps in the hope of apprehending someone. There were heated exchanges on TV, with the DA being projected as either a conscientious, responsible public official or a publicity-hungry, big-office-seeking busybody. Whether it worked wonders for the DA's prospects remained to be seen.

Meanwhile, the whole episode came down heavily on Bodega. Wall Street noted that Bodega and its customers had run into significant *legal* problems, and that was all that was needed for an analyst or two to downgrade the stock and a few potential clients to withdraw their plans, which prompted another wave of downgrades by the analysts. And on it went.

SOMETHING ROTTEN IN THE STATE OF CALIFORNIA

ON A SLOW NEWS DAY, the local television stations reported that the problem had started when an upscale spa in Palo Alto—with the usual European-themed decor and the obligatory Asian-sounding, monosyllabic name—ordered some apples online. When the apples arrived at the Qi spa, they placed the fruits in the large crystal bowl in the lounge. A hungry guest picked up an apple and complained that it was a tad soggy. It didn't help that the Qi staff failed to address the problem immediately. And it didn't help at all that the customer knew someone in the press.

The *Palo Alto Post* picked up the story and ran it with the headline "Health and Wealth: how to lose both at the 'happening' places." The story went on to say that the so-called upscale spas weren't upscale at all. They cut costs everywhere and bought subpar goods at the lowest possible cost. Why, they even ordered their fresh produce *over the Internet!* Case in point was Qi, prominently featured in a sidebar.

There was a follow-up story in the *Cupertino Chronicle* titled "When apples turn out to be lemons." Soon a barrage of stories attacked Bodega practically on a daily basis. Talking heads on the television extolled the virtues of "old school" living—the joys of going to the coffee store, sampling coffee and buying it instead of ordering the beans over the Internet. Ditto for wine, produce and pretty much everything else. The stories generally ended on the same note: No amount of technology could replace the human touch.

The human touch soon became the buzzword at dining establishments. Some restaurateurs saw their chance to appear on local TV and get some free publicity: "We never order our produce over the Internet. Everything is handpicked."

"We're caught in a bad news cycle," Eric said. "Sometimes the media people don't have much to cover, so they hang on to whatever they have for quite a while."

He did seem to have a point. It had indeed been a slow news week or two in America, with no celebrity lawsuits, celebrity divorces, celebrity rehabs or celebrity autopsies. The only story was the rotten apples bought over the Internet. It had started as soggy apples, but somewhere along the line it had turned rotten.

"Does anyone disagree with Eric?" Barbara asked.

The meeting room was quiet for many seconds.

"Sam, what's your take on all this?"

"There are no defects in the software. By now we've fixed all the bugs. The real problem seems to be elsewhere, mainly public perception, I think."

"See?" Eric said. "There are no *real* problems. It's all this media noise that's killing us."

"What's the way out?" Barbara asked.

"Why not launch a media campaign?" Sam said. "Let's re-build our image by showcasing happy customers. I speak with some customers from time to time for system stabilization and support, and I know some of them are quite happy. If you like, I can ask for an endorsement."

"That's a *very* good idea," Barbara said. "Let's get this going."

"No," Eric said. "Don't do it."

"Why not?" Sam asked.

"TV spots in the middle of all this bad publicity? No way. We'll end up looking desperate."

"So your solution is to *do nothing*? Just sit back and watch while they chew us up on a daily basis?"

"Yes, I think we should wait it out. There are times when saying anything at all is counterproductive. Like I said, let's wait till it's over. It shouldn't be too long."

"And what makes you say that?"

"Come on, all those TV people can't keep covering us forever. Sooner or later they have to move on. Yeah, we can rest easy the moment they have a 'news flash' about a politician cheating on his wife. Or when a celebrity couple files for divorce. Or a white woman goes missing."

Sam wanted to ask Eric if he could arrange any of that, but he kept the thought to himself.

"Come on, people," Barbara said, "we have to work as a team and brainstorm. What alternatives do we have on the table?"

Nobody spoke a word or even moved. Except George, who had been sitting next to Barbara and listening the whole time. He quietly gathered his papers and left the room.

CASH IS THE NEW PROFIT

GEORGE SAT IN HIS STUDY with a stack of the latest reports. He knew what the numbers meant even before he reviewed the printouts: More was rotten than just a few apples. The *numbers* had started to stink.

He had prepared on containing the financial mess for only so long, till the revenues from New Horizon started to pour in. Once that happened, his plan was to offset his earlier "sale" to South Seas by "purchase" of technology over two or three years from the shell companies that Myeng had set up all over the Far East, while still having a decent profit left at Bodega to show to the street. A fairly circuitous route, but in the end, it would have helped him clean up the books like he had managed to do at Interstate.

But that wasn't going to happen—that was the bad news. And in the world of finance, bad news always came with worse news, and the worse news was that he could end up alienating his friends, starting with Myeng. Even Clara, if he didn't act soon. And if the word spread beyond his circle of friends, it would be all over. In George's world, it was the kiss of death if your name showed up in the newspapers.

Even as his worst nightmares played out in his mind frame by frame, he kept running the numbers, covering one dreadful scenario after another.

Eight p.m.—time to call Myeng. George poured himself a double scotch and practically gulped it down. He looked at his notepad one last time and then called Myeng.

"We need to talk," George said.

Myeng didn't respond.

"Myeng?"

"Is there a problem?"

"I have to say things aren't working out as planned. There's going to be a bit of bad publicity, and—"

"Never mind the bad publicity. I can handle it. Tell me what's really going on. Do we have a problem?"

George sighed. "There's no way to sugarcoat this, Myeng: I've got to restate the revenues, going all the way back to where we started."

Myeng remained silent.

"Myeng?"

"What do you expect me to say?" His voice was perfectly calm, which was far more unnerving than him throwing a fit. "You know perfectly well that I didn't expect this. Not from *you*, George."

George had never felt more out of his element. He remained silent, wondering what to say next. Losing Myeng wasn't an option, not merely because of what had just happened but because of what was about to happen.

Don't blow this, George. "Myeng, I learned something today and I'm calling you at the first sign of trouble. But it isn't over yet, which is another reason for calling you now."

"You can still save Bodega?"

"No," George said. "I can't tell you how sorry I'm, but

Bodega is as good as gone. But I know you trusted me and you took a lot of risk, so let me make it up to you."

"Go on."

"Well, if we can act now and take advantage of your shell companies and short Bodega…"

Myeng remained silent, unnerving George even more. All George could hear was the gentle tapping of fingers at the other end.

"Myeng?"

"Have you planned this all along?" Myeng asked, his voice softening just a little.

"I had to improvise. So what do you think?"

"I don't like where we are now, that goes without saying. But as far as contingencies go, this isn't too bad… I assume you have a plan?"

"Of course. Got a notepad handy?"

"I always do."

"I know," George said, his confidence coming back to him. "Which is why I asked that question. Please throw away the notepad and keep no records at all on anything we do today."

"Go on," Myeng said.

"How many companies do you have in the Far East?"

"More than enough."

"Very good. Then proceed with the shorts. If you route the trades through your companies so they can never be traced to you or me, there is money to be made. Can you wing it?"

"It won't be the first time I'll have done it."

George smiled to himself for the first time that evening. "I really like you, Myeng," he said, reaching for his whiskey. "You simply aren't the type to panic."

"This isn't the time for paying compliments. Many things can still go wrong."

"Yes, yes, my thoughts exactly. The markets are open in Hong Kong, right? And the European markets will open in a while."

Myeng sighed. "This is going to be one long day."

"Tell me about it."

As Myeng executed the trades, George made notes on what to tell Tom and Clara. And on what was next for Bodega.

George stepped into Barbara's office. Uncharacteristically, he wasn't carrying his attaché case or even the customary notepad. He slumped into the chair in front of her desk.

"Barb, you aren't going to like this."

"Oh my God!" Barbara said. "Is it that bad? What happened, George? Are you leaving us? Seriously, we can write up a new contract for you."

What use is a new contract, Barb? Pretty soon you won't have the money to pay me anyway. "Well, there's no way to sugarcoat this: We need to restate."

"*Restate?* This is a nightmare! This is crazy!"

"I know, but that's where we are now."

"How bad is it?"

"We'll wipe out all our profits for three quarters. Restating in itself is pretty bad news. Coupled with the profits being wiped out—"

"Oh my God! I can't bear the thought of our stock plummeting now. I am *this* close to buying a yacht, George. But no! This has been a never-ending nightmare!"

"Look, Barb, we have much bigger problems."

"What can be bigger than *this?* George, you aren't making any sense."

"We're running out of cash. Do you understand what I'm saying? We're running out of *cash.*"

"Oh my God! I'm about to have a stroke, here and now. So you're saying we can't pay our bills anymore?"

"Oh, we can pay them for now, I guess, but not for too long."

"We've got to meet Steve," Barbara said.

"Where is he?"

"Gone sailing, I believe. I'll get to him on the satellite phone as soon as I can. Meanwhile, not a word of this to anyone."

George kept his guard high, even higher than his usual, when he and Barbara were shown into Steve's living room.

"What do you mean?" Steve went pale as Barbara began to speak. It seemed that he had instantly lost all his tan, presumably earned over the course of a week of sailing and sunbathing.

"Sorry, Steve," she said. "Like I was saying, we need to restate."

"I know what *restate* means," he shouted. "But what do *you* mean?"

"Um…"

"You're the freaking CEO, for Christ's sake! I hired you to take care of Bodega and I trusted you with everything. And after all these years, now you drag me out of my sailing trip and tell me the jig is up? That's it?"

"Just calm down, Steve," Barbara said. "It's not all over. We can still manage this if we calm down a bit and act carefully. There are a couple of things I suggest on the damage control."

"Don't tell *me* to calm down, do you hear me?" Steve screamed. "And don't you dare suggest a thing to me. I've had enough of your suggestions!"

"Steve."

"I'm not finished! In fact, if we all can 'calm down a bit and manage it carefully,' why don't *you* calmly manage it from your office? You're supposed to be the freaking visionary, right? And you, George. You're supposed to be the freaking financial genius! Why do you even bring it to *me*?"

Barbara fell silent.

Steve continued to scream. "Is this why I invested millions? Is this what I hired you to do? Is this why I supported you no matter what you did?"

"But, Steve—"

"I've heard enough. I've got to talk to the board. Now get out, you two. Do you hear me? *Get out*."

George and Barbara walked into the emergency board meeting Steve had called. Nobody smiled at them or shook hands with them, and many even declined them the courtesy of eye contact. George wasn't sure if they were angry about how things had taken a bad turn at Bodega, were worried that their names would now be associated with Bodega's demise, or were merely upset that they had to cut short their business travel or golfing vacations or sailing trips or whatever the heck they did with their time.

Steve was no longer screaming. He spoke in a quiet tone befitting a sober board meeting, even when he addressed Barbara, but his words were deadly. He thanked her for her services to Bodega and terminated her on the spot and appointed Ted as interim CEO.

Then it was time for agenda item 2: termination of George's services.

"Now, George," Steve said, "there's no excuse for how you managed the finances."

"I'm confused," George said. "You didn't get the message from Jane?"

"What the hell are you talking about?"

"Ah, I see you aren't in the loop. But that's okay, in the general scheme of things, it isn't all that important."

"What?"

"I got an update for you all that you might care to hear." George spoke in an uncharacteristically forceful manner, stopping anyone who was about to speak with an impatient hand gesture. "I've been watching Steve's entrepreneurship at close quarters for many years, and I must say I've grown a bit jealous of his drive and ambition. So after much thought, I've chosen to leave Bodega to pursue my own entrepreneurial ambitions. My formal letter of resignation will be reaching you soon through proper channels."

"That's baloney," Steve shouted. "You quit so we couldn't fire you."

"You aren't happy about how things turned out, I know. But once it's all done and settled, I'm sure you'll see it differently. Good luck, everyone, I gotta go."

Without waiting for any response, George left the room. He didn't even have to go back to his office to pack up his things. He'd done it hours before.

George called his wife on the way home. "Honey," he said, "I quit."

"*You quit?* I thought you said they could fire you any moment."

"Yes, which is why I quit."

"Thank God it finally happened, one way or another. You've been all tensed up for so many months... So it's all over?"

"No, that's not what I said. I said I quit—I didn't say it was all over."

"Must you speak in riddles all the time, George? For once, can't you say something simple and clear?"

"Okay then, let's go out to dinner today. There—I said it. Something simple and clear."

She hung up on him.

Accounting 101

Sam couldn't believe or even comprehend what he'd heard: Bodega was going to restate its revenues. Restate? What did it mean, specifically?

His confidence hit a new low as he approached his team and asked the question: "Guys, does anyone know what *restate* means? Oh, I know it's bad news, but what does it really mean and why are we doing this?"

"It means we falsified our financial results all along," Jennifer said.

"But we *were* making profits, right?"

"No, we were reporting profits, but we weren't making money."

"That doesn't make sense. Making profits *is* making money. You speak as if those are two different things."

"They ought to be the same, but they aren't. So here's what it boils down to: *We are going to report our past revenues all over again.*"

"I still don't get it, so let me ask it differently: Why are we doing this?"

"Because we flat out lied," Vick said. He seemed to be catching up faster than Sam could manage. Kris, meanwhile, seemed to be taken aback almost as much as Sam was.

"Just what does this mean?" Sam asked. He was trying hard to articulate his thoughts, but try as he might, he was overcome with the feeling that he didn't know enough even to ask the right questions.

"We were making book profits, not *cash* profits," Jennifer said. "It was fake numbers all along."

"You keep saying that over and over, but it doesn't make sense. How can people lie right in the face of the internal audit, board members, external auditors, Wall Street, the SEC, maybe even the IRS—who knows?"

"I know," Jennifer said. "But we lied. That's the simple truth."

"Since you seem to be the know-it-all here, let me ask you a basic question: Do you remember the basic math we all aced before taking up calculus? Old McDonald had a farm. He bought a cow for a hundred dollars and later sold it for one fifty. He made fifty dollars profit. So what happened now? Did Old McDonald ever have to restate his revenues? Are his stock options underwater now?"

"Old McDonald did all right," Jennifer said. "Because, you see, he sold the cow to a neighbor for *cash*, not to South Koreans on easy credit."

"But—"

"You see, just like the 'final version' of software that we ship right on schedule but keep fixing thereafter, corporate profits aren't always as final as they sound. It's something they send over to Wall Street right on schedule and then keep patching up or 'restating' as needed, just like software. Of course, they don't call it the Third Quarter Financial Results Version 2.0 Service Pack 1, but that's what it really boils down to."

Sam was prepared to argue that all corporate profits were measurable and final. Turned out Jennifer was prepared to disabuse him of that idea.

"Say you spent a dollar and bought a lottery ticket this afternoon," she said, "and tonight they announce the winner on TV. You find out that you won a million dollars! So you go to the lottery office in the morning to claim your money, but holy moly, you realize you lost the ticket somewhere. You know, just somewhere. Too bad, huh?"

"Go on."

"So how much did you lose?"

"A million, I guess," Sam said.

"A million it is. But get this—if you never checked the lottery results on TV and you misplaced your lottery ticket anyway, I bet you wouldn't think much of it. It's like you lost a dollar."

"Okay, but—"

"So what did you lose, Sam? A dollar or a million? Your profit or loss doesn't depend on what you bought or sold or spent or lost. Your loss is entirely based on whether you watched TV tonight! Not so simple, right?"

Sam thought hard for several seconds but couldn't think of a counterargument. "But I thought numbers don't lie," was all he could say.

"Yes, but people can lie about the numbers."

"I've been looking it up on the Internet all day," Vick was saying later that day. "I believe that sometimes the book profits are good profits, too. I mean, it's not like *all* book profits are the wrong kind..." He trailed off when Sam and Kris looked at him blankly.

Sam turned toward Kris. "Did you have these fake profits back in India?"

156

"I was expecting that. Whenever something unusual happens in America, you guys have to ask me that. Like, 'Hey, Kris, do kids in India bring in a machine gun and shoot up the whole school?'"

"So, in the end, do you have scandals or not?"

"I don't know, but what makes you think that you Americans have a monopoly on dishonesty? It's been a while since everything went global."

"That's comforting!"

"But, at least where I worked—at Vizag Turbines—the results sucked all the time. I guess they were honest people. But you know what's cool about Turbine Research Academy, where I once wanted to work?"

"Go on."

"The TRA is a government agency, so nobody is ever asked to make a profit. It's all funded by the government. You guys get it? No obligation to make a profit, *ever*."

"Wow," Vick said, "sounds like you got an advanced civilization over there."

"Yeah," Jennifer said, "government is the ultimate helpdesk. You have your fun and the check is on the state."

"I still remember their offer," Kris said, shaking his head.

"And what made you give it all up?" Sam asked.

"Well, the day I got that offer, I was reading an American business book—*Odyssey,* I think—and I had to ask myself: Do I want to spend the rest of my life designing turbines, or do I want the chance to change the world?"

"See?" Vick said to Sam. "You probably never realized it, Sam, but you aren't alone in your quest to change the world."

"Say what you want," Kris said, "but to tell you the truth, I am a bit scared. I need a job to keep my visa active. I have no family here. There's no way I can call an uncle and borrow some money."

"Yeah, like we all have uncles that will gladly lend us money," Vick said. Before Kris could react, he added, "Sorry, dude, I didn't mean to be hard on you. My point is, we don't have a helpdesk either."

"What do we do now?" Kris said.

"Let's wait and see," Sam said. "Barbara or Ted should be sending out something pretty soon."

There was a press release the next day that said the impact of restating the revenues would be "significant." That bit of ominous news, which made the rounds among the investor community at Internet speed, wiped out whatever residual value Bodega's common stock had had.

Later, a company-wide e-mail from Steve said that Barbara and George were no longer with Bodega and that Ted was the new CEO.

"Ted?" Sam said.

"Is that how low Bodega has fallen?" Vick said. "We once crowned him the professional slacker, for God's sake."

"But on the other hand," Jennifer said, "when it comes to never taking the responsibility for anything, this guy is a natural, so he's got that going for him."

A few hours later, a company-wide mail from Ted said, among other things:

> The impact of this restatement is going to be, like we communicated earlier, significant. While the re-statement goes through the due process, we will be pursuing various opportunities aimed at boosting operational efficiencies even as we continue to place a premium on responding better than ever to the changing market needs.

"Does anyone know what this psychobabble means?" Sam asked.

Vick provided the translation: "We suck. We are a bunch of liars. And we are going to lay off a lot of people."

Paradise Lost

It was a development that was at best a yawn to the rest of the world but a real shocker to the people who were affected. Everyone at Bodega had feared it at one time or other. Many had had an occasional suspicion or two. The cynics had seen it coming all along. But when it finally happened, no one knew what to do. From the youngest rookie to the steadiest executive, everyone was looking at everyone else for direction.

The only ones who seemed to know what was going on were the security guys. They walked around telling people what they could take home and what they couldn't. The HR guys were nowhere to be seen. A few top guys, including Ted, could be seen fretting about, but as ever, they were of no use to anyone.

As the reality started sinking in, people hurriedly walked across the aisles and jotted down friends' private e-mails and other contact details. Many stood in their cubicles shaking their heads in disbelief. A few shed a tear or two.

In a while, everyone started trooping out, carrying medium-sized cardboard boxes into which they had clumsily stuffed their personal items. Many were calling home to deliver the bad news. Some even started calling recruiters then and there.

"Wow, this is it?" Sam said. "They send us home just like that?"

"What did you expect," Vick said, "a hug from Barbara on the way out? Oh, wait—she got sacked last week. That's why you don't get that goodbye hug and kiss."

"No, but a 'thank you for all the hard work over the years' kind of speech from some higher-up would have been nice. Or a brief e-mail message from Steve."

"Dude, we have been on life support for far too long." Vick said. "When they finally announce we're all going to die, what do you expect, flowers by the bedside?"

"No," Sam said, "but a kind word from the doctor delivered in person would've been nice. Instead, I caught the morgue workers filling in the paperwork for my autopsy and that's how I learned my fate, know what I mean?"

They kept walking, vaguely uncomfortable about leaving the workplace without the laptop or the security badge. They stopped at a poster that said, "On our Balance Sheet, we have just one Asset: Our Employees." The poster was barely a month old, but it appeared to be from a different era.

"Why are you walking so slowly?" Vick asked. "Do you think this is all a movie where they show us leaving the office in slow motion? You know, with wailing violins in the background? Get real and walk faster."

"Dude, if you really must know, I'm not in slow-mo. It's just that this cardboard thingy of mine is heavier than yours."

"That's because you carry a lot of baggage," Vick said.

"Very funny."

Sam stuffed his things into his car and walked over to Vick's car.

"So what's next?" Sam said. "Where do we go from here?"

"Bowling," Vick said. "I haven't bowled in a long time."

"Come on, that's not what I meant."

"I know. Seriously, man, I feel relieved. I've been living with this pain for months and months. Now that it's all over, I'm feeling better, you know?"

"Yeah, like a cancer patient who just died and has no pain to feel."

"That's one way to look at it."

"And what's the other?"

"After years of pain and several near-death experiences, the patient has become a free soul. Yeah, that's how *I* look at it. So what do you expect me to do, man, mourn my demise or celebrate my free soul?"

"Whatever. I'm going home now. I gotta think this over."

"See you tomorrow," Vick said. Then he added hastily, "No, I don't mean here at work. How about Joggers Trail, around noon?"

Council of War

"My dear fellow citizens," Vick began amid weak smiles from Sam and Kris, "just when we got around to changing the world, our lives have been overturned, our paradigms have shifted, our cheese has been moved and if you can think of any other tired clichés, they've all happened as well. *But…*"

"I like the 'but' part of it," Sam said. "So you got something for us?"

"No," Vick said. "That was where I was going to hand it over to *you*. So, you got something for us?"

"Yes, I do."

"Can you say it twenty words or less?"

"No, I can't. Seriously, I think Bodega folded not because of New Horizons but *despite* New Horizons. Yeah, I still think the idea was fundamentally good. And I think someone out there must be doing something similar to New Horizons and they might value our experience."

"I see where you're going with this, but I got a news flash for you: Most people aren't hiring."

"Vick, we don't need 'most people' to hire us. We just need *one* company to hire us. In any case, we have one more option."

"Which is?"

"Look, we *have* developed and deployed a whole new solution. Can't we get a bank loan or VC funding and do it all over again? You know, start a company?"

"Looks good on paper," Vick said, "but you don't seem to have thought your cunning plan all the way through."

"What do you mean?"

"Which banker will lend us money? I mean, with Bodega on our resumes! What kind of management skills have we got? Two weeks ago none of us could tell honest profits from fake profits. I know *I* still can't tell the difference. How good are we going to be at running a business?"

"Well, since we aren't good at accounting, we won't intentionally cheat. And that isn't a bad start these days."

"Try telling that to a banker," Vick said. "Mind if I go with you? I've never seen a banker laugh."

"Dude, I was only making a point," Sam said.

"And your point has no merit. You're trying, I give you that. But I think you're too fixated on New Horizons. You gotta break free."

"I see. So *you* got any good ideas?"

"Good ideas? No, I got a *great* idea: Let's go to Duncan's and get wasted."

As they started walking, Vick turned toward Kris. "You haven't spoken a word. What's going on?"

"It is a big blow," Kris said.

"I know," Vick said.

Kris shook his head. "Sorry, but I don't think you do."

"Dude, we're in the same boat here."

"No," Kris said. "I'm here on a work visa, and so I *have* to be employed at all times."

"What?"

"I *have* to work in tech in order to live here. So if I don't get a job soon, it's all over for me."

Vick stared at Kris in disbelief. "That sucks. Sam, did you hear that?"

Sam didn't reply. He was thinking about what Kelly had told him the night before.

"You want to start a new company?" Kelly had said. "You know what kind of a toll it will take on you? Sam, you know you haven't taken a break in years. How long will you keep killing yourself like this?"

"Look," Sam said, "I'm just throwing up some options here."

"Options? Why is killing yourself with work an option? And why is getting a life *not* an option?"

"Kelly, there's no reason to be upset. I can handle this."

"Of course I have a reason to be upset! Has it ever occurred to you that it wasn't just *you* that had high hopes for this project? I always thought that once New Horizons is done, you'd slow down a bit and—"

"Kelly, I really don't need this now. I just lost my job and I—"

"So at least *now* you can get a life. That's my point. You need a break. *We* need a break. What hurts me is that you *still* think of your project as the most important thing ever."

"I'm sorry, but you're mixing things up here. Look, we *will* take a break, and you *will* get to meet my family. But I have to work on what's next. You know how important New Horizons is to me. I was finally doing something useful with my life and then it slipped through my hands at the last minute. I have to get it back. I've already failed once. To give up now would amount to giving up once and for all."

Kelly remained silent.

"Kelly?"

She didn't reply. Sam remained silent as well, wondering what to say.

"I got a flight to catch," she said at last. "Let's pick this up when I'm back in town."

"Sam, did you hear that?" Vick was saying.

"What?"

"It's the worst of all dilemmas, really" Kris said, putting his beer down on the table. "As an Indian living in America, do I resent losing my American job to Bangalore or do I cheer my country taking on the world?"

"Wait till your checking account runs out," Vick said. "When you're hungry you'll know which side you're on."

"You have a point there," Kris said. "But on the other hand—"

"Oh, there's another side to this?"

"Seriously, I'm with Sam on what he said earlier. Finding a job is important, but we shouldn't go after *any* job that's out there. You have to be passionate about what you do. Otherwise, what's the point of working?"

"Yeah, you gotta chase your dreams," Sam said. "If you don't, one day you'll wake up only to realize you've wasted your whole life. And yes, anyone who did something worthwhile *has* chased a dream. I know you don't see it that way, Vick, but then, the line between dreams and follies is quite thin."

"So your plan is to chase one folly after another till you're 70? Dude, you gotta settle down a bit and take stock."

"Come on, Vick, what's life but a series of inspired follies? Haven't you heard that before?"

"Yes, I remember that line from *Pygmalion*," Vick said.

"Fittingly, it works only in books. I don't think life works that way. For starters, where's your helpdesk?"

"What?"

"Anyone who did anything cool had a helpdesk," Vick said. "And I don't mean that professor dude in *Pygmalion* or those NASA dudes who put a man on the moon or even the alleged workers of the alleged Area 51. Look at those guys who sail around Antarctica or climb the unnamed peaks in Alaska. They *all* have sponsors. In fact, it all goes back a long way, guys. Yes, it does—even Columbus had a helpdesk, you know, the Spanish queen who sponsored all his high-seas fun."

"So?" Sam said.

"I'll take a job, any job," Vick said. "I don't need a cool job."

"Any job?"

"Any job."

"Even outside tech?"

"You bet," Vick said. "I'll do whatever it takes, but I will stay employed."

"Seriously, *outside* tech? What will you do?"

"Opportunities are everywhere. I know it's a cliché, but some clichés are actually true. Let me give you an example. You've been to the gym, like, a hundred times this year. Have you even paused to see how a gym is run? Oh, no, you *have* to be in tech!"

Sam and Kris looked at each other and burst out laughing.

"You want to own a *gym*?" Kris said.

"But in his defense," Sam said to Kris, still laughing, "two-thirds of America is fat or obese, so a huge market is out there waiting for Vick's new venture. But—"

"But what?"

"I'm not into these things. If I'm doing something at all, I want it to be worthwhile."

"What about you, Kris?" Vick asked.

"You speak as if I have a choice. What have I been telling you all day? I *have to be* in tech."

"Sorry dude," Vick said. "This is my third beer. Can you blame me?"

"Funny," Sam said, trying to cheer everybody up, "how we reach out for a drink when things are really good *and* when they're really bad."

"What's the big mystery?" Vick said. "In victory you deserve it, in defeat you need it."

Sam raised his glass. "You have a gift, my friend."

"Dude, I was just quoting Napoleon."

"Way to go," Kris said. "You shoot him down when he quotes *Pygmalion* and then you get all classy and quote Napoleon."

Yes, I Want Large Fries With That

GEORGE POURED HIMSELF A SCOTCH in a self-congratulatory mood.

He had died a million deaths in a month. Indeed, the only time he'd smiled that month was when Myeng told him the two of them were making real money by having bet real money to cover the possibility that fake money would soon be discovered to be fake money.

While most of his short trades were executed through Myeng's companies and the rest were done through Clara, George had gradually sold off his "official" holdings in Bodega in the months leading to its fall, on the grounds that he "wanted to cash out my earnings to pursue my entrepreneurial ambitions." Given that his resignation letter said pretty much the same thing, it had all fallen into place—the risk of getting caught by the short-staffed SEC was minimal to nil.

As for Bodega's board members, George wasn't worried—one half of them were Barbara's buddies and the other half were Steve's sidekicks. Fat chance *they* would get to him.

Yes, the scariest moments of his life were behind him.

***

Myeng had made a bundle for himself, and every time George called him, he sounded more cheerful than ever. But George suspected that Myeng had taken a severe lashing from his bosses on account of the Bodega deal and the resulting bad publicity. He didn't want to alienate Myeng—as a group vice president at South Seas, his access to the big piles of cash over there was going to be better than ever. After some deliberation, George made the usual call.

"So," he asked, "do you want to get back into the game?"

"Maestro," Myeng said, "I'll gladly reinvest every single penny you made me."

"I'm not talking *your* money," George said. "We need South Seas money."

"Do you care where your capital comes from?"

"Yes, and that's because we're kicking it up many notches. This is a much bigger game and we need *lots* of money."

"A much bigger game?" Myeng said. "George, you're driving me nuts! Didn't we just make a bundle?"

"You've never heard of supersizing?"

"Okay, okay, I get it." He laughed. "Yes, I want large fries with that. And a half-gallon soda, American-style!... So, what's on the menu?"

"Real estate," George said. "Do you think you can talk to your guys? The idea is a simple, but there's money to be made...for them and for us."

"Wow, this time around I don't have to explain *anything* to our guys. Any idiot can be sold on real estate."

"I'd say. By the way, there's no bad blood between the big guys and you?"

"No way! I'm Myeng the risk-taker, not Myeng the idiot! Why do you even ask?"

"Never mind," George said. "So you're in?"

"What's not to like in real estate? God doesn't create any more land. Ask any South Korean living in a crowded city."

"And government doesn't allow any more construction. Ask any Californian living with zoning restrictions."

"When do we start?"

"Got a notepad handy?"

"I always do. Let's start."

A Year in the Wilderness

As the ethereal notes continued to play in the background, Sam lay in bed wondering what time it was. For a moment he wondered if the music was disturbing his neighbors. He reached for the remote to turn the volume down, only to realize the notes were playing in his mind, not on the stereo.

It had been weeks since he had bothered to clean his apartment, met Vick and Kris for drinks, worked out at the gym, looked for a job or otherwise showed any signs of normal life. Day after day, he lay in bed, tossing and turning, wondering what had gone wrong, fending off the occasional depressing thought, and telling himself that things would get better. But no matter how much he tried, there was no denying the reality: Kelly had left him.

She had sent him an e-mail, and that was it. "You wanted to change the world, Sam," it had said. "I admired you for it and I still think the world of you for having such a goal. You may not realize it, but it does have a downside—why, it took me a long time to see that downside for myself."

He had read it a hundred times. Every time he read it, it

hurt more. And every time he read it, he kept promising to himself that he wouldn't read it again. But he kept reading it, and he always fell apart at the same lines:

> There are two ways to ruin any chances of leading a happy life. The first is to chase a goal twenty-four hours a day, day after day, and gladly give up all the little laughs and joys that life has to offer in exchange for that ever-elusive moment of jubilation. The second way is far worse, in that it NEVER fails. You know what it is, Sam? Falling in love with someone who chases a goal twenty four hours a day.

Sam looked at his cell phone. Another voice mail from Vick.

"Dude, this is getting crazy!" he said. "You've *got to* start working again. I'm telling you for the millionth time, my boss is hiring and he could use a good geek or two. Call me back even if you don't want the job, do you hear me?"

Sam erased the message and looked at the bookshelf across from his bed. There they were, all the journals he had kept since he was 13. He picked up a recent journal and started reading: "When the dotcom went belly up, I thought I emerged wiser. Now, after all these months I'm back to Square One all over again but none the wiser."

He read older and older journals, sometimes skipping many pages, and felt disproportionately old when he read his first entries on Pandora. Though it had been a little more than two years, it seemed as if he had written them a generation earlier.

He finally reached the very first entry he ever made: "Today Mom gave me a journal to keep. But I don't know what to write." Sam couldn't help but smile, and for a moment he reflected on his happy childhood.

For someone who hasn't done much with his life, I've written quite a bit. Wait—written quite a bit?

He sat up as an idea took shape in his mind. After months of inactivity, and thanks in part to Vick's relentless voice mails about every tech opening he had come across, Sam came to the realization that he had to get things going sooner or later. He hadn't found anything exciting to do, but what if he started a blog on the new economy and shared his thoughts about what he had been through? He already had all the material he needed right there in his journals.

At the very least, it would keep him occupied. And who knows? Maybe, just maybe, it could open new doors.

Sam switched on his laptop and started typing out a piece titled "Mystery House."

Sam started working out at the gym. Though he was there to get some exercise, he couldn't help but think about what Vick had once said about working out at the gym all the time but never noticing how a gym was run. He started paying a little attention, more out of curiosity than anything else.

What he learned wasn't especially encouraging. Most gyms were struggling, and they made the largest chunk of their profit from clients who paid their monthly dues on auto-pay but never bothered to show up and use the gym. Put simply, the profit was coming not from the use of the service but from the non-use.

Sam researched businesses benefiting from customers' inactivity or laziness or mistakes and learned more: The DVD-rental companies made a good chunk of their profits from late fees; the credit-card companies made a fortune on sundry fines and penalties; the airlines' margins were highest on ticket changes and cancellations.

So the key to running a successful business in America is to sign up a customer and pray he'll somehow screw up? Whatever happened to the business model of making a profit from doing something of value to the customer? Wait—is that the reason why New Horizons didn't make money? Instead of doing our best to help our clients, should we have screwed them over from day one? No, that doesn't make sense.

Sam paused and looked at what he had written. Yes, with a bit of rework he could post it on his blog.

Sam looked at the new message. It was from Frederick, an on-line "friend" whom Sam had never met, requesting that Sam call him as soon as he could.

"Sam, it's nice to talk to you finally," Frederick said when Sam called him. "Hey, it says on your profile that you are currently between jobs, and that's the reason I wanted to talk to you. There is a vacancy here that you might be interested in."

In the days that followed, Sam signed up as production support manager at Oceania Telecom, a broadband company located in Sunnyvale. Granted, it was an average job. His performance was measured by how smoothly the system ran in any given month and by how quickly he closed the occasional "showstopper" ticket.

Nobody said a thing about changing the world, in or outside the office or anywhere in the Valley anymore. Silicon Valley had gone from the best of times to the worst of times in a span of three years and descended into an era of collective resignation where employers barely paid what it took to keep employees from leaving and employees barely did what it took to keep employers from firing them.

As the months rolled by, there were occasional updates from the Bodega gang. Sam was happy to hear that Kris had managed to find a job in Palo Alto and had married a girl his parents had chosen for him during a brief visit to India. But Sam was even happier to learn that Vick and Jennifer had been seeing each other and were about to get married.

"Finally I can say one good thing came out of Bodega," Sam told Vick.

"Thanks," Vick said, "but your blog isn't too bad either. And you seem to have quite a following."

You Can Always Restate It

GEORGE KEPT THINKING about Barbara as he drove to the club. "Far too many things are going wrong," she had told him over the phone, "I really need some advice. From someone who's on my side."

George wasn't sure he was on Barbara's side or for that matter anyone else's side, but he had no problem with Barbara thinking of him that way. He'd agreed to meet her so she could pick his brain, as she'd put it.

Even without Barbara's giving him all the details, from what he had gathered on the cocktail circuit, George knew what was going on. The way he saw it, Barbara was paying the price for having kept too high a profile when things were going well at Bodega. She had leapt to the front and hogged the spotlight at all the events. She was the only person from Bodega who'd granted interviews to the press, she'd attended industry conferences and made the occasional keynote speech, and her name had been prominently mentioned in every announcement from Bodega. Many at the office had resented or even become a bit demoralized by her behavior. But then, who could speak out against the boss, particularly the one the business press was fawning all over?

With a business press that had trouble telling a press release from a researched article, the "visionary" stunt hadn't been too hard to pull. For starters, she'd been a "thought leader" who delivered keynote speeches at industry conferences, and covering her at those conferences was fun and therefore newsworthy. Whenever the press would run a story on "power women," her picture was bound to show up in the sidebar.

But when Bodega folded, the only thing that dropped faster than Bodega's share price was Barbara's press coverage. The press corps simply moved on to the next engaging story about another upcoming power woman. Then it got worse: The business community quickly dubbed the failure of Bodega as *her* failure.

For her part, Barbara fought back employing the usual tools of the trade: power lunches at fancy places, press releases, leadership profiles in tech journals, the works. Through her publicist, she kept claiming that a massive turnaround had been well underway before she was let go.

For many a month, Barbara tried to get one of those big-time gigs she had always considered to be rightfully hers: $20 million to sign up, $20 million a year to show up and $20 million as a parting gift if she screwed up. But with the stigma of the Bodega failure always showing up next to her name in Google searches, that was one hard gig to land.

George parked his car and walked into the club, where he found Barbara waiting for him.

She was all smiles. "Could we get you a scotch? I think they've got a few single malts from the Speyside."

"Thanks." He was flattered that Barbara remembered what he liked. "How's it going, Barb?"

She started pouring out her woes, which amounted to more or less what he had heard or expected. "You have a knack for managing things when they go bad," she said, "I was hoping you would have some advice for me."

No, Barb, I can manage a bit when things are about to go bad, not when they're already bad. He sipped his drink in silence. As he saw it the question was "How does one restate a failure?" A pretty hard thing to do. In fact, a lot harder than restating the revenues. But on the brighter side, subjective reinterpretation of one's past was protected by the First Amendment; the SEC had no control over it. *The First Amendment?* Yes, of course, that was it! He looked at Barbara, who looked back at him eagerly, as if he was her only hope.

"I got three words for you," he said.

"I can't wait."

"Write a book."

"What?"

"What you've got here is an image problem, Barb."

"That's what I like about you, George. You always cut through the bull. Yes, of course I have an image problem."

"A barrage of press releases or public appearances won't do the trick. If anything, that will make you look desperate. A bunch of friendly interviews on the television won't help either, even if you can arrange them. What you want is a medium where you can say your piece and you're in complete control of the content. A memoir."

"But, George, I've never written anything."

"You'll need a ghostwriter, that's all. That can be easily arranged."

"That's it?"

"No, you'll also need a publisher, which is a lot harder to arrange, but I have a few contacts. I'll see what I can do."

"You know someone?"

"Long story. Everyone owes everyone else a few favors. And there's a guy in publishing who owes me one."

"Oh, George, the best thing I did in a whole year was to call you this morning."

"Glad I could help. And please be careful about what you write in your book. I mean, don't project yourself to be kind or compassionate or gentle or anything like that. That's what *men* should do. Women should be tough."

"Really?"

"You bet. Men should project themselves as visionary and kindhearted. Women should project themselves as tough and intelligent. That's how memoirs work. I know that sounds crazy and sexist, but that's just how it is."

"I have no problem with that. I *am* tough, George."

"Of course. So, what are you going to call your book?"

"Well, we've just started. I haven't thought of anything yet."

"Just a suggestion: Call it *Tough Girl*. It's all about you— how you stood up to a discriminatory male-dominated world. Make that your story more than anything else."

"But I don't have a whole lot to say from a 'woman's perspective.'"

"Then make up something. No matter what your book is about, your readers will see you as a woman first. Anyway, once you've got that angle covered, elaborate on how you tried very hard, in the face of strong economic headwinds, to save Bodega. How you provided steady leadership in choppy waters."

"Good advice, George."

"Don't hold back anything. In fact, you should make it clear that there was a massive turnaround already underway at Bodega but the board threw you out prematurely—it would have been quite a different story if you'd stayed on."

Barbara kept nodding enthusiastically. It wasn't just that she was in agreement—she seemed to actually believe in it.

"I'll leave you with a last piece of caution," George said. "There are no guarantees that the book will do the trick, but that's the best option you've got. And if you need anything, anything at all, call me."

"Thank you, George."

As he drove home, he found himself doubting that the book would do the trick. While the setbacks, disasters and downfalls in other walks of human life could always be reinterpreted as "adventures" or "challenging times" or even "moral victories," failures in the world of business didn't go by any other name.

"Wow, that was unusually generous of you," Clara told George later that day after he'd brought her up to speed.

"Not at all," George said. "Everyone owes everybody else a few favors. Now she owes me one."

"Come on, she's all finished. What can *she* offer you?"

"Her silence," George said. "As long as she thinks I'm on her side, she'll keep quiet about anything I did at Bodega."

"Ah."

"Bottom line, I don't want to see my name in the newspapers."

Clara laughed. "You suck!"

"Tell me something I don't know."

Waiting in Line

For three years, tech has been going everywhere and nowhere, but nobody really knew what was going on. Every once in a while the press touted "the next big thing," but it always turned out to be a false dawn. But, slowly but surely, the mood across the Valley is changing...

"Dude."

Sam stopped typing and looked across the table. Vick was standing there with his customary day-old stubble and a collarless white T-shirt that said "Got Motivation?"

"Kris is on the way," Vick said. "So what's up?"

"Oceania is hiring and I want you and Kris back on team."

"Changing the world all over again?"

"More like waiting in line. Things are looking up for sure, and when the next big idea hits us, we gotta be there. Bottom line, if you aren't waiting in line, you'll miss the show."

Vick's face fell. "I see."

"What's on your mind?"

"I'd love to work with you again. And before you ask, I really don't like my job all that much."

"Then what are you waiting for? Listen, I spoke with my boss. The interview will be just a formality. We'll even match your pay."

"No, no. Here's my situation: Jen is working on something she always wanted to do, and—"

"Oh, she started her own charity?"

"No, but she joined one—the Caring Hands Charity. She's super-busy, juggling her new career and the baby, but she's happier than she's ever been. I made a promise to her: I'll stay put for a couple of years while she gets her things in order."

"But I'm not asking you to take a pay cut or anything."

"No, man, it's like… I owe it to Jen to keep things *stable* for her. My job sucks, but I know they'll keep me around for a while. I can't give up *that* for anything else at this point."

Sam remained silent for a moment. "I see," he finally said. "So you're Jennifer's helpdesk now?"

Vick smiled. "I haven't thought of it that way, but yes, I *am* her helpdesk, and happily so. And why not? You could live your whole life chasing an ideal if that's what makes you happy, or you could just sit back and support someone with an ideal and be almost as happy. I'll take the second option any day."

Sam didn't reply.

"Tell me," Vick said, "do I have a good thing going or not?"

"What's this 'good thing' you speak of?" Sam heard a familiar voice from behind. Startled, he turned and there was Kris.

"Sam is hiring," Vick told him.

"Cool," Kris said. "Sam is the best boss I ever had. Oh, wait—I hope you aren't expecting *me* to join you."

Sam looked at Kris. *Is he in or is he out?*

"Dude," Vick said to Kris, "you're sending some mixed signals here."

"Long story, man," Kris said, dashing Sam's hopes in an instant. "But I'll keep it short. One word: *immigration*."

"I don't get it," Sam said. "After all these years, your petition is still pending? How long is this going to take?"

"GOK."

"What?"

"God only knows. Just so you know, the immigration queue can get so long that they have no choice but to close the line and say, 'Your category is not current.'"

"So you're waiting for the line to open up so you can start waiting in line?"

"Yeah, that's pretty much how it works. Don't even get me started on my wife's situation."

"I don't believe it," Sam said. "The INS guys are still giving you a hard time? After all these years?"

"First of all it's DHS, not INS. And no, *they* aren't giving me a hard time. If anything, they were actually nice to me when I ran into some issues. My problem is with the immigration *law*. You might think I'm splitting hairs, and I don't want to trouble you with my problems."

"That's weird," Vick said. "No offense, but I know dozens of guys from India at my office who don't do anything other than undercutting my pay. *They* all got their green cards and we have *you* waiting in line."

"It's a long process, and it didn't help that Bodega folded and I had to switch employers. Anyway, I don't want to trouble you guys."

"Seriously, dude," Vick said, "have you considered going back to India?"

Kris looked away and remained silent for a few seconds. "I

have a dream, too," he said. "Perhaps not as noble as MLK's, but a good one nevertheless... I want to do something big. Something *original*. That's why I came here in the first place."

"*This* is the place?" Vick said. "I don't know what you've been smoking, but I want that." As eyebrows rose, he hastily added, "I meant metaphorically."

"I'm not judging you, man. Just curious," Kris said.

"But how long will you wait? Do you really think things will work out for you?"

"I think I'll hang on for a while. But on the bright side, I'm already in the right place. If anything cool happens, I expect to see it here first."

"Dude," Vick said, "you're *so* sold on the bright side of America."

If Anything Cool Happens, You'll See it Here First

THE SIGNS HAD BEEN FLASHING all over the Valley for the better part of two years, but in retrospect Sam could see that he had missed many of them. All signs pointed to the second coming of the Internet: Six years after the dotcom bust, the social networking sites were a roaring success, user-generated content was here to stay, and everyone was blogging about everything, including what other bloggers were blogging about their blogs, stopping just short of bloggers blogging about their own blogs.

As always happened in the Valley, the developments in the virtual world trickled down to the real world. Traffic around the Valley picked up, flights out of San Jose became pricier and the labor market seemed to tighten up just a bit, at least to the point where employers no longer took applicants for granted. But the first real sign that made Sam sit up and notice was as virtual as they came.

It started with the television broadcasters' shifting to high-def and therefore "vacating" the frequencies they had used for their low-def broadcasts. And, of course, the vacated frequencies ended up on the auction block. The situation was similar to what happens to a piece of real estate freed up by new zoning laws. In fact, it was all so *last century* that the auctions didn't merit a mention even in the business press. But these particular auctions did come with a twist: A portion of the frequencies was to remain "open access," readily accessible by any Internet-enabled device.

Quite a few geeks around the Valley noted it on their blogs. If—and like always in the Valley, it was a very big if—it all came through as planned, a small spectrum of airwaves would no longer be managed as it had always been. For a good month or two, many speculated about how this could lead to "truly open" handhelds. New applications could be written and deployed, anything from baseball tickets to airline tickets to calling for a taxi. In the end, it created quite a buzz among the geeks, but all that buzz was nothing compared to what came next.

Sam stood transfixed as he laid his hands on an iPhone for the first time. It wasn't just because of the cool factor or even the form factor. Just like the early ads promised, it didn't deliver a "kinda sorta Internet" or a "shrunken version of the Internet"—it delivered *the* Internet. For the first time, a major player was delivering a full-blown browser—not the WAP simulated apology of a browser that he had earlier worked on but a *full-blown* browser—on a cell phone. A full-blown browser meant that the constraints he had faced on New Horizons were all gone, and the touchscreen meant he could get far more creative with the navigation. But in the end, it also meant many others might be thinking exactly what he was thinking.

Even after patiently waiting for the upturn for so many years, Sam often felt unprepared for what was happening.

Things began moving frighteningly fast, like a bear that had been sleeping for months only to wake up one day and sprint across the valley.

"Vick, it's obvious," Sam said. "We had a false dawn before, but this time it's for real."

"Thank you for the Zen moment, master. Would you care to elaborate?"

"Let me ask you this: What was wrong with New Horizons?"

"Man, it's like asking why the Roman Empire fell."

"See, it's all coming back, isn't it? Cell phones weren't good enough. Technology wasn't mature enough. Signals weren't strong enough."

"Ah, I see. Since none of that is true now, it should work this time around. So it's New Horizons all over again?"

"Only way cooler," Sam said. "I have three words for you: *Timing is everything.* It happens all the time, you know that. Somebody tries an idea and it bombs in the marketplace; everyone calls it 'dead on arrival' and moves on. For years nobody gives a damn, and then *someone else* exploits all that good work and makes a ton of money. You *know* that happens all the time. Now it's happening all over again."

"Someone is writing an app for groceries? I don't think so."

"No, no, I don't mean just groceries. I'm talking mobile commerce. Movie tickets. Weather. Real-time stock quotes. Location-sensitive ads. Or it *could* very well be groceries. *What* we sell isn't important. What matters is…*the time has come.*"

"That's one way to look at it."

"What's the other way?"

"I've seen this movie before, and I know how it ends."

"Oh really? Let me give you yet another way of looking at it: A good idea isn't something you can casually brush off in five minutes!"

"No, I'm serious," Vick said. "In fact, I think *you* gave it all of five minutes."

"Oh, really? What have I missed?"

"Have you stopped reading the news? Just when you and I think tech is coming back, *the whole freaking economy* takes a nose dive. Remember how Bodega went down? Now imagine the whole country going down! Sam, do you really think people are going to pour money into tech at a time like this? In the middle of this greatest-disaster-since-the-Great Depression thing?"

Sam smiled.

"What are you smiling at?"

"I knew you would say that," Sam said. "But I've done my homework, dude." He handed him a business card from Allen Ford of Panamint Technologies.

"You know this guy?"

"I've been talking to him for a while," Sam said. "He's very nice and professional, and he's hiring."

"Okay, but—"

"Let me throw in a little Occam's razor," Sam said. "I'm with you on the whole economy-takes-a-nose-dive bit, but as long as *someone* is hiring us and paying us good money, all that big-picture stuff is really secondary, don't you think?"

"That was more of an Occam's chainsaw," Vick said. "I'll need a minute to think of a comeback. But let's talk Panamint first. What's going on?"

"I've applied for project manager. They said they'll interview me in a week or so."

"Good for you."

"They also need an architect. Looking at the job description, I thought you would be the best fit, even more than Kris or Jennifer... Oh, how is Jennifer? What's she up to these days?"

"She's all right, working on—"

"Um, you think she'd be interested in—"

"Dude, you're all over the map. Lay off Jen for a minute. So you want me to apply to Panamint? Man, it's been years since I've sent out my resume."

"Oh, brush it up a little and send it over. How long is that going to take?"

"No, man," Vick said, "all this is a bit out of the blue. I gotta think it over and talk to Jen. I don't know how stable or dependable the Panamint job is going to be. My job sucks, I know, but it's *safe*. In this economy, you really have to think about these things."

"Yeah, safe, stable and dependable," Sam said in a tone that clearly surprised Vick. "Vick, can't you hear yourself? You keep telling me your job sucks. But what do you expect? As long as you keep chanting 'safe job, safe job,' it will continue to suck. With all due respect, do you know what will become of you when you put up with mediocrity for years and years in the name of job security?"

"Look, if you want to call me names, just come out and say it. Really, dude, *mediocrity?* I didn't expect *that* from you."

"It's not about calling names or scoring debating points or how big your paycheck is. This is about *why we live.* Let me ask you this: When was the last time you laid in bed all night too excited to sleep because you kept thinking about work? When was the last time you believed you were doing something useful with your life?"

"Sam—"

"Remember how you and I used to work till midnight

and still couldn't wait to come back to work first thing in the morning? Seriously, man, have you just *given up*? Do you want to live the rest of your life looking back at what you did in your *twenties?*"

Vick didn't say anything.

"Vick, most people get *one* chance in life to really do something. One chance to rise above everyday mediocrity and actually *do* something. Now life is giving us *two* chances, barely six years apart, right where we live. So when our dream is finally coming true, you want to run away from it? Be honest—are you really the type to sit back and watch the world go by?"

Vick was quiet for a moment. "Let me think it over."

Rock Stars Needn't Apply

George was having a good time. He was on the way to Panamint Technologies to attend a meeting. The meeting in itself wasn't significant—the agenda items varied from the reassuringly normal to the predictably boring—but it was George's first meeting after his recent board induction.

He had accepted the directorship a month ago. It happened after Clara introduced him to board Chairman Dave Richardson. While the introduction had opened the door for George, it was his "considerable experience in being the steady hand in a chaotic new economy company" that got him the seat on the board.

"We *are* pretty chaotic," Dave told George when he signed up. "When it comes to big-picture issues, we look to you for sound guidance in the best interests of Panamint."

As he pulled into the parking lot, George looked at his watch. Not too soon, not too late. Time for the meeting—and time to make that favorable first impression.

"Moving on to the last agenda item," Dave said, "review and approval of Panamint HR policy." He turned to his vice president of HR. "Lou, what have you got for us?"

"It boils down to the basics really," Lou began. "We deal with a pretty complicated suite of technologies, and some of these technologies are still a bit nascent. We need people who are bright and who can adapt, and the HR policy is built around just that. So, gentlemen, before I share the details, any comments?"

George realized Dave and a couple of the other board members were looking at him expectantly. He cleared his throat, took out his Blackberry and checked it before looking up and smiling at Lou. "Oh, I'm sorry, I was just checking to see if we were still in the nineties." Everyone laughed, much to Lou's obvious embarrassment. "Lou, if I've learned anything at all from my years in the industry, it's this: In the end, a business needs a few sensible people who get the job done. Nothing more, nothing less. I don't know about you, but believe me, I've been there and I've learned my lessons."

"But, George—"

"I'm not finished! Take it from me, the success or failure of Panamint will ultimately depend on how well you manage your resources. So, first you establish clear goals and budgets. Then you make a list of skills needed for each project and hire *adequately competent people at the lowest possible cost*. I'm going to be blunt: Getting all romantic about 'best of breed' isn't going to help you one bit—we don't need rock stars. We're running a business here."

"We're running a business here" was a sentence George had found very effective of late. It was a simple and undisputable truth, and by association, anything that was said immediately before or after it also qualified as indisputably true. George was aware of the curious leap of logic there, but on the other hand, it always worked.

"Lou," Dave said, "it appears that the HR policy needs a bit of rework."

"Um, Dave," Lou said, "we kinda started following this policy already. I told Allen, Peter and the others to go ahead."

"What?"

"You know, I was hoping that the board approval was going to be a mere formality, so I already circulated this policy."

Dave looked at George.

"Okay then," George said, "you go talk to them and undo the damage you've done so far. It's still early in the day for Panamint, and you guys have this golden opportunity to start with a clean slate. Just don't start on the wrong foot, all right?"

Nobody said another word. As everyone trooped out, a few members of the board and some of the senior managers stopped by to shake hands with George and make a few approving noises while Dave watched and smiled.

George left the meeting with exactly what he wanted.

The Resurrection

Sam wasn't worried about the interview. He felt as if he had been preparing for it for years. The only thing he wasn't sure about was what to wear. After some deliberation, he decided to forgo the obligatory suit and tie in favor of business casual. Wearing a suit and tie to a job interview would make him look desperate. He wanted to look *cool*. As in "I'm the man for the job, but I'm not all that keen."

But as he waited in the lobby for his turn, he started to get the feeling that it was going to be a tough sell. For starters, there were two other candidates for the job, and they were both wearing formal suits. As the minutes continued to pass well beyond the appointed time, Sam waited patiently for his turn. He had applied for the position of project manager, after all—patience wasn't just a useful trait in that position but a fundamental job requirement. Eventually, he was shown into a meeting room.

"If the marketing guys demand fifteen features to be delivered in two months," he was asked, "how will you respond?"

"I'll ask them to prioritize."

"What if they say they're *all* must-haves?"

"Then I'll look them in the eye and say, 'Well then, *I'm* going to prioritize them for you.' That usually gets them moving."

"Well done. So, can you tell us what makes or breaks a project?"

Easy. "Support from top, committed project team…"

Fifteen minutes into the interview, it all degenerated into small talk—always a good sign. Sam tried to make the right noises, commenting that heavy commuter traffic around Cupertino was an unmistakable sign that the economy was picking up and so on.

"We'll be in touch, Sam. There's going to be a second round but that's just a formality. The senior veep likes to meet everyone before they're hired for a quick chat."

Sam left the building with a sense of hope he hadn't felt in years. He was sure Vick's interview would go well, too.

As he drove right through a stop sign and an old man yelled at him, Sam realized he was getting ahead of himself, and he dragged his thoughts back to his immediate surroundings.

Sam checked the time: 2 p.m. Time to call Vick.

"Remember, dude?" Sam started as soon as Vick picked up the phone. "You claimed you've seen this movie before. So how did it go? I told you these guys were different!"

"You sent me to the wrong movie, but the ending is the same."

"What do you mean?"

"Man, I've never been more pissed in my whole life," Vick said. "A couple of low-level idiots asked me a bunch of low-level idiotic questions, that's about it. Not a single question had any substance. It was all about some stupid checklist they'd drawn up."

"A checklist?"

"Yeah, these guys came into the room with a 'list of skills' they'd drawn up for the job. They were going line by line, asking me if I used this language, that tool, whatever. Once they checked everything off, it was time to leave."

This makes no sense. Whoever interviewed him didn't get the memo on how to hire. "What's the point of it?"

"*You tell me,*" Vick said. "A cursory reading of my resume would have answered all their questions."

"There's been a mistake, I'm sure," Sam said. "They're a start-up and these things happen. I'll talk to Allen and find out what's going on."

"Don't bother."

"So you're closing the door based on something that lasted all of ten minutes?"

"That the interview lasted all of ten minutes *is the problem.* A job interview is a two-way street. When they're judging me, I'm judging them, too. You, of all people, should know that."

Sam sighed. "So you want out?"

"Yeah, like they wanted me *in* at some point. I never stood a chance, Sam, I'm telling you. I could tell it from the moment I walked in."

"You could tell that from the moment *you walked in?* Hmm… Is it possible that *you went in* with that frame of mind and naturally it all ended in bad vibes?"

"Are you kidding? I *was* indecisive when you told me about Panamint, but that was two weeks back. Sam, when I went in today I totally wanted the job. The only reason I don't want this job now is that I don't like to work with ignorant, self-centered idiots. So I'm not the problem. Stop analyzing *me.*"

"Okay, okay. I get it. I'm calling Allen to find out what's going on. Obviously there has been a mistake. I'll get back to you soon—this afternoon, I promise."

"I'll be at Duncan's a little after 5. See you there."

As Sam hung up, he noticed a text message from Allen asking him to call ASAP. *There it is—one good sign in the middle of all this confusion. They always want to talk to you if you're hired. Otherwise, they send you an e-mail.* While the phone rang at the other end, he played over what he'd say about Vick.

"Sam, I have some bad news," Allen began.

Sam took a deep breath as the news sank in. He had aced every question in the interview. How *could* someone else beat him out?

"Well, it happens," Sam managed to say. *But this makes no sense.*

"I hope there are no hard feelings. I really shouldn't have dropped you into this."

What does that mean?

"I shouldn't be telling you this," Allen continued. "A lot of office politics got in the way."

"I see."

"But I called you for a totally different reason. There's something I want to discuss with you confidentially."

"I'm coming over," Sam said.

"We can't meet in our office. You know the coffee shop opposite Panamint?"

"I'll be there in fifteen minutes."

"Things haven't been the same since they got this 'finance whiz' to join the board," Allen said, dropping two sugars into his coffee. "He doesn't know the first thing about software, but he gets to rewrite the rule book around here. Can you believe it? Yeah, every idea now has to go to the bean counters for approval. And this is what completely pisses me off: George

Stevenson governs from his freaking boardroom and never talks to anyone."

My God. "George Stevenson?"

"Yes. You know him?"

Sam stared at Allen. *George works at Panamint? And he's the reason I didn't get the job? What have I done to him to deserve this much spite after all these years?*

"Sam?"

"Did George tell you not to hire me?"

"You know him?"

Do I know him? No. Even though we worked at the same place for years, I never felt I knew the guy.

"In any case," Allen continued, "it's not like he said anything specifically about you. It's his new *policy* that killed your prospects. Sam, things aren't the same around here anymore. I feel the difference every day. And you know what? I've had enough. I'm leaving Panamint."

"You're leaving Panamint?" *Why are you telling me this?*

"I know some VC guys. Which is why I wanted to see you. Just forget about George and his stupid HR policy and all about Panamint. *I* want to work with you. And if you and I can put together a team, we'll have a good chance with the VCs. Let's do something on our own."

Sam looked at him in disbelief. *Panamint is nothing compared to this... Finally, things as they should be—a small team of like-minded people with VC backing. No office politics. No bean counters. The whole team working diligently day and night.*

"It may sound silly now, after all these years," Allen continued, "but I don't mind telling you. When I came to Silicon Valley ten years back, I wanted to change the world—nothing less. After all the hits and misses all these years, believe me, there's still a part of me that wants to make a real impact on the world. In fact, things are better now than ever. The market is mature, the technology is stable, and I've made a few contacts in the Valley. This is my real chance to do what I always wanted, Sam. This is more than just a business to me. That's why I want to get some good people on my side."

My God.

"The VC guys have been asking to see a team before making a final decision on funding. I've been talking to them for weeks, and I have to tell you, my time is running out a bit. We need at least two more people soon, assuming you want to take the plunge, of course."

"Two people?" Sam's mind was still racing. "I think I can help."

"That's *very* good. If your friends are anything like you, it's a done deal. I *knew* you'd come through, Sam. You know, from the moment I met you, I could tell you were a dependable man… God, I can't get over what Lou did to me today. He sided with George and backtracked on everything he promised in a matter of hours."

"This may seem a little off-topic," Sam said, his heart still racing. "Do you know a good immigration lawyer?"

"That's hardly off-topic," Allen said. "I know exactly where you're going with this. Anyway, yes, we can do an H1 transfer. If your friend is on EAD, that's even better."

God, this is getting better by the minute.

"So what do you think?" Allen asked.

"I want to give you a pleasant surprise. It won't be long, I promise. Can I call you around 10 tomorrow?"

"Call me any time," Allen said, beaming at Sam. "Nothing is more important to me than this."

They shook hands and Sam practically ran back to his car, eager to get in touch with Vick and Kris. He picked up his phone and saw that he'd missed a call from Kris. He called him back.

"Sam, can we meet soon, this evening if possible? I really want to talk to you."

"No, no," Sam said. "I'm coming over to your office right now."

"What?"

"*I* really want to talk to you."

LAND OF OPPORTUNITY

"I GOT IT ALL FIGURED," Sam said. "We can transfer your visa or even GAD—"

"You mean *EAD*," Kris said.

"Yes, yes," Sam said. "Allen will take care of all that."

"Allen?"

Sam filled Kris in on what he'd been up to, never pausing to catch his breath. It wasn't until he'd finished that he noticed something was amiss with Kris. He looked uncharacteristically downcast.

"You know why I wanted to meet you?" Kris asked, practically in tears. He looked away, trying to compose himself, then turned back to Sam. "Brace yourself. I'm leaving America."

"What?"

"It's all over for me, man. Seven years after I started calling America my home, I'm still a 'temporary worker,' with my green card nowhere in sight. I'm leaving."

"*That's it*? Are you going back to India?"

"No, I'm going to Canada."

"What?"

"I filed my papers for Canada six months ago. They just approved my permanent residency and I'm leaving."

"Kris—I can't believe it, man. *You're leaving?*"

"I'm tired of it. Seven years, man. Year in, year out, I lived here and paid every single tax like any American citizen, but… but I'm not sure if I can *live* here, let alone vote. Yeah, all this in a country founded on the battle cry of 'no taxation without representation.'"

"Kris, Kris, you need to calm down a bit," Sam said. "All this is quite a change, man. What happened?"

"*Nothing* happened! And that's exactly the problem. My immigration petition is exactly where it was."

Sam stood speechless, unable to believe what he was hearing, unwilling to bring up Allen again. The idea of Kris leaving Silicon Valley, not to mention America, was way more upsetting than anything else at the moment. "Kris! You're leaving Cupertino for Canada?"

"British Columbia is no match for Silicon Valley, I give you that, but the Canadians do it differently. They are careful about whom they want to admit, and if you qualify, your permanent residency is approved in a matter of *months*. Now I can live in Canada and do what I want, and that goes for my wife, too. That's what I call the land of opportunity—"

"Kris!"

"I thought about it over and over. The system is broken. It didn't work for me. And you know what? It isn't working for you, either."

"What?"

"Look, immigration was *supposed to be* all about people with rare skills. Instead, what do you do? You take in 85,000 H1Bs every year like clockwork, no matter what the state of your economy, and complain about how it's killing *your* careers, all the while leaving *our* lives in limbo… All I ask is this: Be clear about who you want to welcome to America, and be quick and efficient about it. Is it really that hard? Anyway, it's all a moot point now."

"Kris," Sam said, "tell me, who's going to hire you in Canada?"

"Haven't you heard? People are hiring all over the world. Microsoft is hiring in Canada. IBM is hiring big time in India and China. In *China,* Sam! American companies are lapping up the best engineers everywhere, and rightly so. I won't be surprised if the next Silicon Valley shows up 9,000 miles away from Cupertino."

"God."

"Things have changed a lot since the market went down. Really, *everything* changed, including how people look at me. You know what? I'm sick and tired of being constantly typecast by everyone from grocery clerks to coffee-shop baristas as a low-wage brown man who makes a living by undercutting the American worker. *I'm* not that. What am I supposed to do, walk around with a hard copy of my W2 to show everyone I'm top-dollar?"

"Is there anything—anything at all—that'll make you change your mind?"

"No." Then he added with tears in his eyes, "Don't get me wrong, I'll never forget what America has done for me. But I can't ignore the simple truth. My contract with America is broken and I'm leaving."

Sam hugged him. "I feel for you, Kris. After all these years, it must be really hard to pack up and start your life all over again."

"But I have hope," Kris said. "That's one thing America gave me."

DUDE, WHERE'S MY BAILOUT?

"WHISKEY," SAM SAID.

Vick's eyebrows rose.

"Whiskey."

When Vick came back, Sam practically gulped his drink down. "Vick, I gotta ask you something."

Vick looked at him and put his glass down. "Go on."

"I want you and Jennifer to come and join us—I mean Allen and me. I know it has been a hell of a day, and you may not think this is the best time to discuss it, but I gotta act, man. I gotta act soon. Otherwise I'll regret this day for the rest of my life."

"Well…"

"Look, it's happening finally. No more office politics, no more bean counters. Kris is gone, man, I told you. But I really need you guys to come and work with me again."

"Jen *isn't* coming back," Vick said. "That just isn't happening."

Sam stared at Vick as his words sank in. *This afternoon, the best-paid engineer I know told me he's leaving America. Now I hear that the smartest person I've known isn't coming back to tech.*

"Sam?"

"Jen isn't coming back, ever? That's it? Vick, you are an engineer, for God's sake. *You* worked with her for years and you know—"

"She's happy doing something she likes," Vick said, "and I'm not about to interfere or let anyone else interfere. I owe it to her, man. And that's the reason why *I* can't come and work with you either. Look, it breaks my heart to say this…"

Vick isn't coming? Vick!

Vick sighed. "I know how much this means to you. I'm sorry… Sam? Sam, are you okay?"

"I can respect Jen's choice. But *you*?"

"Sam—"

"You're not happy with your job, you said so yourself. You don't like your boss, you said so yourself. And you *were* open to working at Panamint, and now you decline a *better* offer from Allen?"

"I would've gladly taken the Panamint job if they made an offer this morning," Vick said. "But that was before you told me about George."

"George I can understand, but Allen?"

"I can't work with Allen either. In fact, I don't even think of it as a better offer."

"That makes no sense!"

"Don't you see it coming? Allen is *doomed,* man. And so is his venture."

"You've never met Allen and you don't have the foggiest idea about anything he does. How can you say that?"

"Because he didn't have the guts to stand up to George today, and that seals the fate of everything he's about to do. Believe me, sometime down the line when he goes to the VCs, he'll meet another George. If Allen gets all worked up and starts any of that 'vision and mission' talk, the bean counters will tell him to shut up and get the costs under control."

"But why does he have to give in?"

"But he gave in *this morning*," Vick said. "Look, if Allen couldn't stand up to the bean counters as a senior manager at Panamint, with a secure job and good pay, there's no chance in hell he'll stand up to them as an entrepreneur anxious for capital. Don't think for a moment your troubles will be over the moment you steer clear of this one George."

"Vick—"

"New Georges are born every day. They're all over the place. Oh, you don't agree? Okay then, prove me wrong. Tell me why your new friend Allen, whom you've known all of two weeks, won't turn out to be yet another George in disguise."

"What?"

"Yes, tell me what's preventing Allen, a man who spent a whole freaking decade in the Valley working his tail off without making much money for himself, from finally 'getting it.' Tell me what's preventing him from making us work round-the-clock, overpromising everything to the VC guys, selling it all to the highest bidder and walking away with you and me holding the bag. Believe me, I've seen it happen. So tell me, Sam, what have you got on Allen that would make me give up what little I've got going for me and join this new team?"

"Have you lost all faith in people? I mean, here's the chance of a lifetime and… How can you brush it off like that, man? Do you know how it feels to hear you talk like this?"

"Do you know how *I* feel?" Vick said.

"You? *You're* the one who's walking away."

"Oh, you have no idea how upset I'm."

"What?"

"You think *you* had a hard day? Do you know what *I've*

gone through for two weeks? I was living my life for what it was worth, you know, having made my choices in life, till we met the other day. You really shook me up that evening, man. I couldn't sleep at all that night, and I thought about what you said over and over for *days*. Then I felt… For the first time in years, I thought I owed it to myself to do something with my life, not just sit back and watch the world go by."

Sam looked at Vick. For the first time since he had known him, Vick was red-faced, fighting back tears.

"I really thought we were going back to our glory days," Vick said. "I wanted to work with you again. I wanted to be young again. I wanted to *dream* again. When I went in for the Panamint interview, I gave it my hundred percent and then some. I thought I was going to have it all. Then you tell me what happened. I *knew* it would turn out this way. Now I just feel *naïve*. I should've seen this coming."

"How *could* you have seen it coming? Vick, you're—"

"It was all an illusion, man. A two-week-long dream. It was, you know, being *happy*—happier than you ever were—only to wake up and realize it was all a dream. Waking up from that kind of a dream can make you so sad that you begin to hate that dream."

"Vick, Vick, you gotta pull yourself together, man. Don't *give up* like that."

"No man, you don't get it. I've been thinking for a long time, even before you told me about Panamint. It all runs much deeper than you and me and George and Allen. The likes of you and I don't matter one bit. It's like *America* told us, 'You guys don't matter.'"

"Vick!"

"America is all about George and his buddies, man. All those big people—the rich guys, big-shot bankers, mortgage lenders, hedge-fund managers, God only knows who else—they can drive this country to the brink of complete meltdown, but they get bailed out. They all go to Washington and get a helpdesk. But, seven years ago when *we* took a licking, they called it 'capitalism at work.' And when *they* fail, they scare America into coughing up a trillion dollars overnight."

"Vick, I—"

"You know what? Next time something like this happens, *I* want to be in on that racket. Oh, why wait for it to happen? Let's call George right now. Let's work with George, bring Panamint down and make some money!"

"Vick, you sound as if—"

"You still don't get it, do you? It isn't the wild wild West anymore, Sam. The villains of our time are a new creed. There are thousands and thousands of them all over the place. But we never get to face them. We never get to talk to them. We never get to question them. And yet, what they do behind closed doors affects our lives in more ways than we can possibly imagine."

Sam didn't speak. He kept playing Vick's words over in his mind.

Several drinks later, Sam and Vick stepped outside and started walking back to their cars. As they walked through the familiar environs of San Bernardino Avenue perhaps for the thousandth time, Sam kept playing his years in the Valley in his mind, wondering what was next.

"There comes a time in everyone's life," Sam remembered his father telling him once, "when you look back and ask yourself what it is that you've been doing with your life. Sometimes you even realize that whatever you've been doing, you've been doing it all wrong. Dead wrong. Son, you want that realization to hit you when you're 70? Or 50? Or when you're still young, with your whole life ahead of you?"

So, that's it? Has life proved me wrong when I'm still young, not once but twice all over? Is this a blessing I've received twice, or is this the kind of blessing that no one should ever be granted more than once? And how does it all end—is it wiser to make peace with the world and take life as it comes, or is it nobler to forge on, in relentless waves of hopes and dreams and follies and failures till the very end?

Sam was more shaken than ever. He walked next to Vick in total silence, even as the questions raged in his mind, with no answers in sight.

"Sam," Vick was saying, barely walking in a straight line, pointing at the familiar office building on San Bernardino Avenue, "remember what it was like when we started? We were heroes, man. We had goals. We had *dreams*, man. We could dream all night long and every morning we came in and worked on everything we dreamed up... Sam, do you remember what you always said? You said Bodega was our helpdesk... Do you remember?"

Sam looked at Vick. He wanted to say something along the lines of how much working with Vick had meant to him, but he couldn't speak a word. The lump in his throat sealed in any words his angst had allowed to escape.

As they neared the end of road, Vick said something that would haunt Sam long after they parted ways.

"The helpdesk is closed, Sam. You're on your own now."

Acknowledgments

Writing a book ought to rank among the loneliest of human pursuits—I mean, it's just the wannabe author sitting alone in his study and typing out a book, right?

Wrong! Despite the fact that only one name makes it to the cover, any published book involves a ton of teamwork from a lot of people (oh, and to think that I took up this "solitary" hobby as a diversion from my usual project management work!).

Given that *CoHD* is my first book and given that it has no backing from a big publishing house (or even a small one), I needed not one, not two, but *three* helpdesks to see it through.

First, I'd like to thank Ravi Obbu and Srilatha Velivala of *Infowave Systems, Inc.*—my employers and business partners for twelve years, which in my line of work equates with something like three centuries. Thank you, Ravi and Srilatha, for your support.

Next, I'd like to thank several competent and helpful folks at *The Editorial Department*—Carol Ruzicka for cover art; Christopher Fisher for interior layout and multiple rounds of editing; Dan Grubb for proofreading; Morgana Gallaway for cover mechanical and e-book layout; Peter Gelfan for initial review; Liz Felix for administrative help; and Ross Browne for his support all through this process. While everyone did a great job, I want to particularly thank Chris Fisher. As a consultant and project manager, I had the chance to work with literally hundreds of competent people over the last twenty years, and Chris is among the best of them, in or out of publishing. And thanks again, Team TED, for all your help.

Last, I'd like to thank Anjana Susarla, PhD—an avid reader and unrepentant lover of books who, among other things, serves on the editorial boards of reputed academic journals—for all her time and help with the concept design, editing and proofreading. The best part is she never charged me a dime for all that help—but then, she is my wife. While on the home front, I want to thank Anna, the wonderful nanny of my twin daughters. Speaking of daughters, they can't read anything yet, but they did give up some of their daddy time, so they do deserve some kudos. Still on the personal front, I want to thank all my friends and family—I'm grateful for your friendship and support over the years. Thank you!